GRACELESS

A TROPICAL AUTHORS NOVELLA

NICHOLAS HARVEY   NICK SULLIVAN
JOHN H CUNNINGHAM   WAYNE STINNETT

DOWN ISLAND
PUBLISHING

Copyright © 2022 by Down Island Publishing, LLC

All rights reserved.

No part of this book may be reproduced in any form or by any electronic or mechanical means, including information storage and retrieval systems, without written permission from the author, except for the use of brief quotations in a book review.

Printed in the United States of America

First Printing, 2022

ISBN-13: 978-1-956026-05-4

Cover design: Harvey Books, LLC

Editor: Gretchen Tannert Douglas

Proofreader: Donna Rich

This is a work of fiction. Names, characters, businesses, places, events and incidents are either the products of the author's imagination or used in a fictitious manner unless noted otherwise. Any resemblance to actual persons, living or dead, or actual events is purely coincidental.

*If one does not know to which port one is sailing,
no wind is favorable.*

Lucius Annaeus Seneca

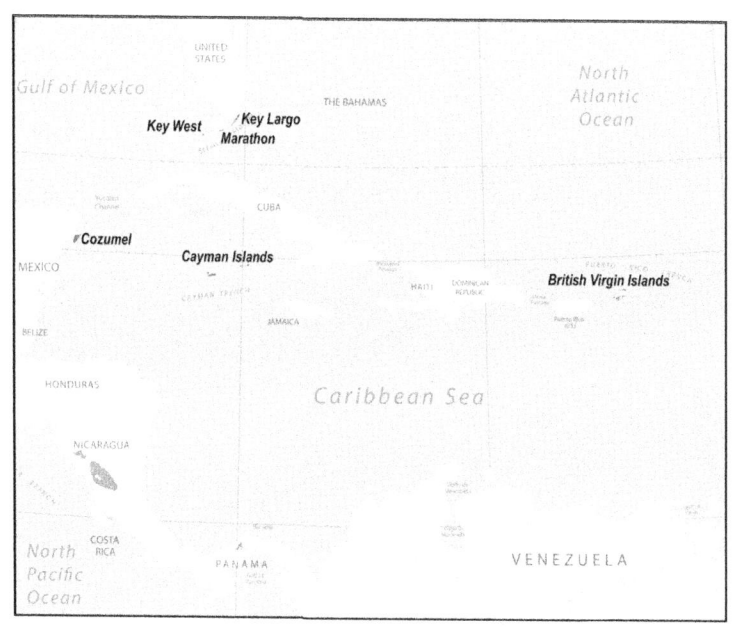

PART I

PROLOGUE

I stirred with a faint trickle of light grazing the wall around the bedroom window that faced the canal. It must have been early, as Bogey, our yellow lab, had yet to bother me for his morning walk. My head felt heavy and my mind cloudy, the kind of haze that came when a few hours' sleep wasn't close to enough rest. I instinctively reached over next to me, and jolted completely awake.

She was still gone.

The events of the past few days flooded back and formed a knot in my stomach, and a lump in my throat. I rolled out of bed and turned on the light. Bogey gave me a confused look from his bed in the corner of the room, and I wished I shared his blissful ignorance. He had seemed lost for a day or two, wondering where Grace could be hiding, but I was still here and his meals came on time, so he'd moved on. I hadn't. I checked my phone. Nothing new. No text messages, voicemails, or emails to explain where my wife could be. I rubbed my tongue across the new crown on the left side of my lower jaw. It was tough to believe that dentistry was responsible for me sitting in our home in Key Largo while Grace was missing somewhere in the Caribbean Sea, but a broken tooth was the culprit.

I made some coffee, because coffee helped everything, and it gave me something to do. I brushed my teeth and stared at the forty-eight-year-old man with slightly graying light brown hair looking back at me. Usually, I passed for forty. Today I could be fifty something. My eyes were baggy with dark circles, and wrinkles seemed to have sprung up overnight. I stopped looking in the mirror.

Bogey was still dragging his feet, so I sat down at the computer and looked at the charts for the umpteenth time. Grace had left Road Town on Tortola in the British Virgin Islands and sailed along the edge of the U.S. Virgin Islands. She'd crossed to Puerto Rico, followed the northern coast, then over to the Dominican Republic where she'd done the same thing, hugging the northern coastline. Three days ago, she'd left the west end of Haiti, heading north to continue up the island chain. Well, that's what she had intended. That's what she'd told me.

Bogey nudged my arm; apparently, he was ready to start his day. I left the computer, which revealed nothing new, and grabbed his leash. It was another balmy, hot day in the Keys, but a welcome breeze met us as we set off down the road toward the park. Bogey quickly marked his favorite shrub by the neighbors' yard, then settled down to trot alongside, tongue already hanging out of his mouth.

I began the same series of thoughts I'd gone over and over in my head for days. Maybe the satellite phone had died or was lost. It certainly wasn't powered up, as it went straight to voicemail. Each and every one of the thousand times I'd tried it. But she should have reached the Bahamas by now, with a string of islands on the way. Plenty of opportunity to go ashore, call, email… hell, a carrier pigeon could have flown here by now. She was a web security specialist after all; if anyone knew how to find a way to communicate, it was Grace. Which suggested she'd been delayed. There was a storm front farther west, but weather in the eastern Caribbean had been fine, so some kind of mechanical difficulty, along with a sat phone failure? It was always the second thing going wrong that turned a difficulty into a disaster. But I wasn't ready to consider any form of disaster, I had to keep my head clear and consider the logical possibilities. At least the ones in which Grace comes home.

The boat hadn't sunk. It could be stranded, but then again, if she was stranded, she would have used the sat phone—unless it was out of service for some reason—so then she would have activated the EPIRB. The Emergency Position Indicating Radio Beacon could be switched on manually, or automatically triggered if the sensor was submerged. It sent a serialized and registered identification code and GPS coordinates through satellites to the nearest ground control station, who would alert the local authorities. And me. Following this logic, the boat was still afloat, and Grace had chosen not to request emergency assistance. Or couldn't.

She had flown down ahead of me to finalize the purchase of our dream sailboat. An Island Packet 380 in our price range—well, nearly in our sworn-to-not-exceed price range—was unheard of, and too good to pass up. I was to fly down a few days after her, and then I bit on an unpitted date. Several days and an emergency crown later, Grace called and told me to meet her in the Bahamas. She'd found a guy that would crew with her for the first few legs, and we would trade spots when they reached Nassau where he was planning to meet up with friends. Brandon. That was about all I knew about him. His name was Brandon. Grace assured me he came recommended by someone in Road Town whom he had crewed for. What if Brandon had fancied himself a nice Island Packet 380? Pirating was far more common than most people were aware; stolen boats and stolen people didn't just happen off the coast of Africa.

We reached the park, but I was already antsy to get back. Bogey finally did his business after sniffing every damn piece of grass for a hundred yards. I bagged his morning gift to the world and dropped it in a trash can as I started back toward the house. Bogey wasn't so keen to get home and looked at me as though I'd screwed him out of his daily ritual. Which I had. Rain or shine, we walked or ran for at least thirty minutes every morning. He trailed behind at the end of his leash, but I couldn't sit around, or walk around, doing nothing any longer. Yesterday, I'd run up a phone bill I'd dread seeing in a month's time, and the only thing I'd learned was there was nothing anyone could do. Not the U.S. police, the Bahamian police, or the Coast Guard. The ocean was too big to search without any idea where to look, they told me. Reaching anyone in Haiti was impossible.

They all asked if we were having marital problems. I was emphatic. I told them no, we're great together. I said that because I believed that, but all this uncertainty and worry was eating me up. Could she have left me? Had my beautiful wife, the woman I was still passionately in love with after twenty-three years, run off with some shit called Brandon? The thoughts wouldn't stop bouncing through my brain and I felt nauseous. The air conditioning in the house and a glass of water helped, but what I needed was something to do that would make a difference.

This was all uncharted territory for a high school football coach. Back at the computer, I brought up flights to the British Virgin Islands. Do I start where she left from, or where she was last known to be? Was she really on the northwest tip of Haiti? That was where she said they were when we last spoke. I quickly realized flying to Haiti and getting to the remote coastline would take days. I needed to start in Road Town, where maybe I could figure out who this Brandon guy was and go from there. It immediately felt better to have a plan.

My phone buzzed and I looked at the text. It was some kind of weird, automated message, not a text from a person. I was about to delete it as junk when I noticed EPIRB buried in the text. Shit, it was from the LEOLUT ground station in Florida. It said the local authorities had been alerted on Grand Cayman. Grand fucking Cayman? I jumped up out of the chair and read the message again. This had to be an error. It couldn't be the new EPIRB Grace had taken with her. Grand Cayman was hundreds of miles west of Haiti, in the wrong direction. Sitting back down, I pulled up a map on the computer and used the measurement tool. Six hundred miles. About the same distance as it was to the Bahamas from Haiti. Three days sailing. Our sailboat, with Grace aboard, had just sunk off the coast of Grand Cayman. I frantically clicked back to the flights tab.

1

I had no idea if I'd covered all the bases, the past few hours had been a blur. I was headed toward a middle seat in the back of the plane on the late-morning flight to Grand Cayman. American Airlines was proud of that seat and allowed me to pay an extortionate price to park my ass in it for two hours. Bogey was having a sleepover with the neighbors who owned his favorite shrub, along with an elderly cat who hissed at all other life forms. Bogey, by default as a yellow lab, loved everyone and couldn't understand why the cat hated him. I was sure he'd get over it if I came home with Grace. The Comfort Suites was the cheapest hotel I could find, and by cheapest, I mean it was a car payment per night instead of a house payment for some of the others. The rental car had been the only pleasant surprise. A local operation called Andy's offered a compact for a reasonable price. I just hoped it was an operational vehicle and Andy wasn't someone with a cardboard sign and a stolen car he was renting me.

I was in complete denial and planned to stay that way

as long as possible. On the drive to Miami International, I'd been constantly on the phone. To my surprise, I reached the Royal Cayman Islands Police Service and was put through to a Detective Whittaker. He was aware of the distress beacon reported that morning and had spoken with someone from the RCIPS Joint Marine Unit who had responded. He was reluctant to share much over the phone and urged me to come straight to the police station when I arrived. He did mention an overnight storm that had finally abated this morning. Whittaker also told me there was no sign of the sailboat, which I was taking as good news.

My next call was strange to make. Grace had worked for CyberWard for nearly ten years, yet I'd never met anyone she worked with. The company was based in Palo Alto, California, and she flew out there once every few months, otherwise everything she did was remote. Her office in the house was like NASA's control center to me, with computers, servers, and everything encrypted this way and that. I understood none of it. My Excel sheet with my players' stats stretched my computer skills, and she often had to help me. I knew she had certain government clearances for some of the work they did, and I'd rib her that she must be Grace Bond. Years ago, she gave a name and number and told me if there was ever a work issue, call that number. Todd Franks in Palo Alto.

It was Saturday, 7:30 a.m. in California, and my call was answered on the first ring.

"Good morning, Mr. Fitzgerald," came a calm, almost monotone voice over the car's hands-free speaker.

"Hi, please call me Nathan," I stumbled. "Is this Todd Franks?"

"It is," he replied, "and I'm sorry we're chatting under these circumstances."

"You know?"

"We are aware that Grace hasn't made contact in several days," he said carefully. "Do you have someone you're meeting in Grand Cayman?"

He knew I was on my way there? I had a creepy sensation that I was being watched or tracked somehow. Was our house bugged, or our Internet usage tracked? Now I felt the need to explain that the buxom German housewives' site was a link sent by a buddy. It would've been rude not to look.

"I spoke with the police there, I'm supposed to contact them when I reach the island," I replied.

"That's good," Todd said. "Would you keep me informed of anything they've found?"

I got the idea Todd would know long before I would, but I obliged. "Of course, I'll call you after I meet with the detective."

"Thank you, Mr. Fitzgerald," he responded pleasantly. "And naturally we have contacted the FBI, so they're monitoring the situation."

"The FBI?" I guess surprise was my main emotion, but I was angry too. I felt stupid. Apparently, I had no idea what my wife did or who she dealt with every day. I suppose I should've been happy that the FBI had an interest in finding her. Hell, bring on the National Guard, the Canadian Mounties and those British soldiers with the big fuzzy hats that guard the Queen. I wanted the whole world helping me find Grace, but somehow the mention of the FBI escalated the situation. I'd been thinking they'd find her and her buddy Brandon motoring into shore in the inflatable dinghy that came with the sailboat. She'd have a rational explanation why they veered six hundred miles off course, and we'd fly home and start arguing with the insurance company. But the FBI involvement suggested something far more sinister.

"It's standard procedure in our line of work," Franks calmly explained. "They may contact you directly."

I had a million questions, but I couldn't piece together a collective thought to verbalize a single one.

"Let's speak again once you're on the island," he continued, and I mumbled something agreeable before hanging up.

If I'd thought it was a strange call to make, the conversation I just had was downright bizarre. I was relieved to make it into the airport parking in one piece as I had no recollection of the last hour of driving. I'd been on autopilot, focused on the phone calls, which was dangerous at any time, but a death wish on the Ronald Reagan Turnpike.

I had a backpack and a small duffel bag I'd hurriedly stuffed with everything I could think of. What do you pack for a "hunting for your missing wife" excursion? I had put in a pair of tennis shoes, some leggings and a couple of T-shirts for Grace. If the boat was at the bottom of the Caribbean Sea, she'd need a change of clothes. By the time I went through security, took the Skytrain, and walked to the gate, my flight was boarding. I was in the "all you other losers" boarding group, so I had time to get a coffee before they let me on. My backpack went under the seat in front, but there wasn't any room left in the overhead for my duffel. There was everything up there from cases and handbags to a large puffy coat, but the flight attendant insisted on gate checking my duffel bag. Who the hell needs a puffy coat flying from Miami to the Caribbean?

I took my seat between a husband and wife who were no strangers to the all-you-can-eat buffet, and I offered to switch if they'd like to sit next to each other. Neither seemed interested, so I guessed we'd spend the flight playing the elbow poke game over the armrests. I paid a shit-ton of money for this seat made for a twelve-year-old; I'd be damned if the Golden Corral couple would steal any of it from me.

Two hours on an uncomfortable plane flight was not the best thing for me right now. The kid in front reclined all the way so the back of his seat was about eight inches from my nose, which ruled out using my computer. I could barely sip my coffee. I'd forgotten to retrieve my headphones from my backpack before we took off and now my six-foot frame was wedged in place like a packet of sausages. I played a game on my phone. Anything to distract me from thinking about Grace, Brandon, EPIRBs and the FBI.

2

I don't think I met Andy, but to my relief his rental car company had a building and lots of cars. The young Caymanian lady behind the desk looked at me sideways when I asked for directions to the police station, but she drew a squiggly line on a map and sent me on my way. The locals had an island accent that was reminiscent of Jamaican, but different somehow. It had an almost musical quality and I realized when I heard them converse amongst themselves, that they were toning it down for my benefit. Which was good because I had no idea what they were saying to each other. Probably, "look at the dumb ass tourist," but they smiled pleasantly, so I smiled back.

It was my first time on the island. I'd caught a brief glimpse from the air as we'd banked on approach. My middle seat had finally allowed me a view of something other than clouds and Mr. Golden Corral's malodorous shirt, decorated with coconuts. Grand Cayman was a tropical paradise straight from the pages of glossy magazines. A magical destination Grace and I could sail to someday. I still hoped.

They drive on the left in the Cayman Islands, a feature inherited from the motherland as a British Overseas Territory. The locals honk loudly and wave frantically when this slips your mind. After fifteen minutes, I arrived at the police station with several reminders.

Detective Whittaker was a tall, slender, well-dressed man in his fifties, with glasses and neatly cropped gray hair. He had less of the local accent, but perhaps he wanted to make sure I was clear on what he told me. He led me to a small office where we sat, and I convinced him I was fine without water or coffee. I had more caffeine in my system at this point than an energy drinks salesman at a Las Vegas convention.

"I'm afraid, as of yet," Whittaker began, "there's been no sign of your sailboat, or your wife and her companion."

I wasn't a big fan of "Brandon the mysterious" being labeled her companion, but I didn't know what term would have sat well with me at that moment.

"I assume you've still received no contact?" he asked.

"No, and I checked with her work before I left, they've not heard from her either." I replied. "Have you sent divers down at the location of the EPIRB signal?"

Whittaker shook his head, "That will be difficult, I'm afraid," he said, and I glanced out the window to remind myself it was a beautiful day outside. The storm had obviously passed through.

"It's rather deep, you see."

Growing up in Florida and living in Key Largo, Grace and I were both advanced scuba divers and were usually underwater once a month or so. We'd regularly dive to over a hundred feet on the wrecks, and the recreational dive limit was 130-feet.

"How deep?"

"Over 800," he replied.

Shit, that was well beyond normal technical diving depths. I mean, divers had gone much deeper than that, but we were talking about incredibly specialized gear and a big operation. They'd be more likely to send down an unmanned submersible known as an ROV—remotely operated vehicle—but I doubted they had one on hand.

"Our islands are the peaks of an undersea mountain range, you see. We have reefs sloping away from the coastline to around 100-feet and then it's like a wall dropping down the side of the mountain to thousands of feet. It's a bit puzzling though," he continued. "The EPIRB was activated for eleven minutes and thirty-six seconds, and then the signal was lost. During that time, it was constantly and steadily moving. We have a trace from the GPS."

"So they were in distress, manually activated it and they went down at the location you lost the signal," I proposed, trying to think it through.

"You would think so, except it shouldn't lose the signal in that instance, should it?" he responded, and he was right.

"The EPIRB should have floated away when the boat sank," I agreed, nodding.

The unit was held in a mount on the outside of the cabin so if the boat sank, the EPIRB unit floated out of the mount and stayed on the surface. The transmitter only worked above water. In that instance, you're looking for the spot where the signal was first activated by the sensor touching the water. It may have drifted from there in the waves and current, but where it was initiated would be where the boat sank. In theory, where the seas take the EPIRB unit was also where they'd take anything else that stayed on the surface. Like survivors. Or bodies.

"Maybe they capsized, triggered the signal, then drifted in the storm and sank where the signal was lost," I babbled, struggling with the fact I was hypothesizing various ways my wife may have died. "The EPIRB became caught in the wreckage somehow and dragged down."

"The storm came from the southwest, but the signal tracked northwest," he replied. "They would have to be motoring to follow that path. I don't sail, but my understanding is they would pull all the sails in and use the diesel engine in those conditions."

He was right again. Whittaker looked thoughtful and gave us both a moment to contemplate.

"What is your guys' theory?" I asked, at a loss where to go next.

He looked at me carefully, "It's possible the unit was activated, and then turned off."

"Why would they turn it on, then turn it off? That doesn't make much sense to me. Grace is an experienced and capable sailor. She knows a difficult situation from an emergency. She wouldn't potentially risk others during a storm if it wasn't a last resort."

"Perhaps they thought they had a problem, and then managed the situation," he suggested.

"Then why hasn't she contacted me?" I retorted. "If they were this close to the island, and sailed on after the storm, why wouldn't she come in a little closer and call?"

Whittaker sighed and I knew what was coming.

"Have you had any problems lately? Disagreements, money trouble, that sort of thing?"

I knew he had to ask, but it sucked. I never thought about the stability of our marriage because I'd never had any reason to question it. In my mind, Grace was the love of my life, and I couldn't imagine being with anyone else. She had never suggested or shown that she felt any differently. Was I in cuckoo land? It was difficult to face up to the fact that I had no idea how sensitive her work was, but the thought that I'd completely misread our relationship was gut-wrenching. Unfathomable. Yet, everyone seemed to be questioning our relationship.

"She hasn't contacted anyone," I said, trying not to sound defensive. "Her work hasn't heard from her, and they have the FBI on the case."

"Yes, I received a call from them. They appear concerned," Whittaker replied quietly.

"CyberWard, or the FBI?"

"The FBI," he clarified nonchalantly.

I was glad everyone else thought having the FBI involved was just another day in the life of your average high school coach, but I was shitting bricks. Back when I played, I was known as a quarterback with nerves of steel. I had the ability to keep my eye on the receivers whatever chaos was going on around me. That was probably why I managed to get steamrolled by a defensive tackle my sophomore year in college. If I'd seen all 255 pounds of him coming at me, I may have avoided the career-ending shattered femur. Regardless, I was a steady hand. An even-tempered, reliable guy that performed at his best under pressure. But this was next level shit.

Whittaker slid a nautical chart across his desk toward me, "Here," he pointed at marks on the water-resistant paper, "this is where the signal was first detected, traveled, and then stopped."

I studied the chart. Having spent my life near, on and under the water, the one thing I could do was read a nautical chart. I checked the depths.

"They were heading toward the island," I noted aloud. "The track almost reaches the drop-off you talked about."

"It does," he agreed. "We estimate a few hundred yards or so."

"The GPS on the EPIRB is accurate to one hundred meters this close to the equator where the satellites are constantly overhead," I said, feeling some hope building as I talked myself into a better scenario. "With the storm moving this way," I continued, pointing perpendicular to the track, "it's possible if the sailboat went down, it was blown in that direction."

Whittaker looked skeptical.

"Move the track one hundred meters east and imagine anything sinking being dragged in the direction of the waves as it goes down." I tapped enthusiastically on the chart. "The boat could be right there, on the edge of the wall in a hundred feet of water."

Whittaker eyed me carefully, and I sensed he was trying to figure out how to let me down easy, without creating a big fuss.

"We have a side-scan sonar unit coming from the States to search the deep water, but it won't be here for a few days. Meanwhile, we've focused our search on the storm path," he explained. "Figuring any wreckage, debris, or survivors, would have been carried that way."

"And what have you found?" I asked pointedly.

"Not a thing. No life vests, boat parts, nothing."

"And what does that tell you?" I fired back.

He grimaced, "It went down really quickly, and likely inverted, trapping everything underneath."

"Exactly," I replied with surprising conviction. "So let's go look and at least rule out that area on top of the wall."

What I didn't say was that my optimism was screaming that a boat going down always deposits debris on the surface. No debris, no wreck. But that was probably wishful thinking. I also didn't correct the man about a sailboat like the Island Packet. With a ballasted keel, it would never invert.

The point was, getting divers in the water would feel like we were doing something, and right then I needed to be doing something that made me believe I'd see Grace again. Hopefully alive. Not finding our expensive new sailboat on top of the wall off the west side of Grand Cayman would be a step in that direction. Or, it'd keep the denial rolling, which was fine with me.

Whittaker took a deep breath and I let him think for a minute. He pulled out his cell phone and looked up a number. Glancing at his watch, he made a call. It was four o'clock, so we'd have three hours of daylight.

"Hello, AJ," he said into the phone. "What are you and Reg up to this afternoon?"

I was hoping he was calling in the police dive team, but now I couldn't tell if he was about to arrange a barbecue gathering for this evening, or we were still looking for my wife. I heard what sounded like a female voice on the end of the line, but I couldn't tell what she was saying.

"Well tell that grumpy old fellow I have police work for you two, and that takes precedence over his Land Rover's oil change."

I reminded myself we were on a small island and I needed to be patient, but this sounded like he was recruiting a couple of amateurs.

"You heard about the missing sailboat, I assume?" he continued. "Well, I'd like to have a poke around and see if we can see anything. I have GPS coordinates."

A poke around was not what I had in mind, especially as my wife's dead body could be what we'd be poking. But at least something appeared to be happening.

"Yes, yes," he carried on after a pause. "Nora's on duty today, so I'll bring her along. Give me thirty minutes to round up a Marine Unit boat and Miss Sommer, and we'll rendezvous on the water."

Whittaker said his goodbyes and hung up, looking at me like I should be pleased. I suppose I should have been, but I was expecting a group of Navy SEAL type guys in all black wetsuits and painted faces. I was confident that's not who'd be showing up.

"She says it's still pretty choppy out there but thinks it's safe enough to dive."

"This is your police diving team?" I asked tentatively.

Whittaker smiled, texting someone as he replied, "We don't have a full-time dive team, but we have a couple of constables who can dive. But for anything technical or tricky, we use Reg Moore and AJ Bailey. They run two of the dive operations here on the island."

I didn't wish to seem rude, but I had visions of a pair of dive guides used to hand-holding tourists around the perfect clear waters Cayman was world-renowned for. This all sounded incredibly rinky-dink. I was thinking of how to phrase my concerns when someone arrived at his office door.

"Ah, Constable Nora Sommer, this is Mr. Fitzgerald," Whittaker said, rising from his seat. "We're meeting AJ in about half an hour to have a look for the missing sailboat. Perhaps you can come along?"

I stood and turned around. Before me was a young woman who looked like a member of the Swedish ski team. Maybe the junior team. Except she was wearing a police uniform. And staring at me sternly with piercing blue eyes as though she couldn't decide whether to tase me or go diving. She didn't say a word. I had no idea what to say either.

"Let's go see what we can find," Whittaker said, and I followed him out the door, shaking my head.

3

Whittaker drove us to the harbor in George Town, which was a natural inlet with a small commercial port on one side and a handful of tour businesses on the other. Between them, the frontage road separated the ocean from a row of shops and restaurants. We parked near the tour businesses and made our way down to a dock where a Marine Unit police boat waited. It was a Rigid Inflatable Hull Boat, as commonly used by police and coast guards around the world. Two powerful looking outboards were hung off the stern and an extended pilothouse left ten feet of aft deck. A large-framed Caymanian man in uniform waved as we approached.

"Afternoon, Ben," Whittaker greeted him. "This here's Mr. Fitzgerald. It's his wife and sailboat that sent the distress call."

I shook hands with Ben, "Please, call me Nathan. Thanks for taking us out."

The man nodded and seemed uneasy about what to say.

He quickly turned his attention to the blonde boarding the boat behind me. I couldn't blame him.

"Afternoon Constable," Ben said with a slight smile.

She acknowledged his presence with nothing more than a brief glance. I began to wonder if she could speak at all. Maybe she had a daily quota of words she was eager not to use up too soon.

Two Marine Unit policemen cast off the lines and we were quickly underway, a light chop in the inlet giving way to larger swells when we headed into the open water.

"I texted AJ and gave the coordinates," Whittaker told Ben, who apparently already had them.

We all hung on tightly, and the boat jolted and bumped across the ocean, faster than I expected. The seas were rough.

"Chopper just came in for refueling again," I heard Whittaker telling Ben, noticing his accent was stronger around the local man. "They'll keep going until dark."

I was on a boat, racing to what was potentially the last known position of the sailboat, and helicopters were deployed, whizzing around the sky, searching the seas. This was better than sitting at home feeling useless.

We were heading north, angling away from the shoreline, and I spotted a white boat coming toward us in the distance. It only took a few minutes and Ben slowed the motors. I was surprised how close we still were to shore; it couldn't have been much more than a quarter mile to the beach. I looked at my cell phone and saw it had four out of five available bars, showing strong service. Grace could have called from the water here. Yet she hadn't.

Ben had called back and forth a few times over the VHF radio with the other boat and they'd switched from the general hailing frequency so they could talk openly. Whittaker stepped outside so I followed.

The other boat was a thirty-six-foot Newton dive special with an open-back cabin, a long aft deck with benches and tank racks, and a flybridge over the cabin. At the helm up top was a large man with a big gray beard and a mess of salt-and-pepper hair blowing in the breeze. A logo depicting a mermaid wrapped around an anchor and an old-fashioned dive helmet adorned the hull with the words "Mermaid Divers." He maneuvered next to us, and the two boats were lashed together with bumpers between the two hulls. Both vessels rolled and swayed in the chop, knocking against each other.

A woman with shoulder length, purple-streaked blond hair stood on the deck of the Newton. She was petite, toned, wore shorts and a tank top, and sported full-sleeve tattoos on both arms depicting artistic underwater scenes.

"Hey Roy," she said, and her soft, cheery voice and English accent took me by surprise.

"Afternoon, AJ," Whittaker said. "Thanks for coming out at short notice."

The woman stepped forward from the stern where she'd tied in the boat and a tall, slim Caymanian man joined her from the bow.

"Young Thomas," Whittaker greeted him, then peered up at the flybridge. "Sorry to pull you away from your Land Rover, Reg."

The big fellow grunted something I couldn't hear and frowned at everything and everyone present.

So, there we were, bobbing on the waves, with the island's crack scuba squad consisting of the Scandinavian Miss Teen cop, who was yet to say a word, the grouchy old sea salt, and the hot chick who looked like the lead singer of a rock band.

"I'll dive with them," I blurted to Whittaker.

He looked at me and shook his head. "That's not a good idea, Nathan, these are not the best conditions, and we don't know what we'll find."

"I'm advanced certified. I have my cert card in my wallet," I pushed convincingly. "I'm more than capable."

"What if you freak out?" the Nordic cop asked, finally speaking, and for some reason I was surprised that she actually did have an accent.

"I won't freak out," I said defensively.

"Ever seen a dead body underwater before?" she countered.

Whittaker held up a hand. "Hang on, Nora."

"Sorry, sir, she can be a little blunt," Tattoos said, leaning against the gunwale and smiling. "But she has a point. We're looking for a downed vessel with the potential of people aboard. That's not something you'll want to see. Let us do it, sir."

They were right of course, but I couldn't stand the idea of sitting up top while they searched the seafloor for Grace. I felt like I was sending my third string players on the field and I needed to take control. I didn't know what I'd do if we did find her; maybe I would freak out. Maybe I'd take the regulator out of my mouth and join her. But I couldn't sit up here.

"I'm part of a search and rescue team in Key Largo," I bold face lied. "I've done this before."

The AJ woman looked like she might be softening, but Blondie was staring at me like I was full of shit. I think she had trust issues. Or really good instincts.

"Show me your cert card, and you can come along," AJ said. "But first sign of trouble and Nora's dragging your arse back to the boat, okay sir?"

Well, at least she was polite with her threats. Maybe that was a British thing. "Nathan," I said, "and my wife's name is Grace. That's who we're looking for."

AJ nodded, "And another fella as well, right?"

I shrugged my shoulders, "I suppose, yeah."

Shit. I felt a pang of guilt. Maybe Brandon was a super guy who genuinely helped us out. His mother was probably worried sick. Maybe he had a girlfriend who was fretting too. But as best I knew, he was the last person to see Grace, and I wasn't ready to trust him or be sympathetic.

We geared up and AJ made sure I was familiar with the BCD—buoyancy control device—she gave me, as well as the regulator and dive computer. It was all nice equipment. We were diving on Nitrox, a gas blend with a higher oxygen content than air. For divers, nitrogen buildup in the body's tissues from the compressed gas we breathed—to equalize with the surrounding water pressure—could cause problems after a while and limit the dive. By using a ratio with more oxygen and less nitrogen, it bought us time at depth before we went into deco. That was when the body's tissues became saturated with nitrogen molecules and you needed to safely get rid of them. That meant going shallower and making decompression stops. It was a bunch of complicated physiological stuff, but the dive computer did all the math for you.

"Okay," AJ started, once we were ready to go. "The storm has messed up the usual currents, so the surface is taking us southeast, but down there it's likely to run straight south along the wall. Reg will hot drop us north of our search area and we'll drift south. If we get down and the current is running opposite, we'll abort and drop again."

She looked at me with a reassuring smile, "Let's go, and hopefully find nothing but reef."

My stomach was in knots. The conditions were rougher than I'd expected, certainly outside recreational diving parameters, and now I was wondering whether making up a story was smart. Then there was the possibility I was about to find my wife's corpse.

"You'll be fine," Nora said, and smiled for the first time. She was stunningly pretty, with eyes that seemed to look clear into your thoughts. "Just don't freak out and we'll be okay."

I was good with "You'll be fine" and the smile, but I guess she thought the last part was reassuring, so I tried to take it that way too.

They had separated the boats earlier as it was too rough to stay tied together, and now Reg moved the dive boat into position. We were all standing at the open transom, hanging onto the handrails by the ladder, waiting for the signal.

"Go!" Reg's booming voice came from the flybridge, and there was no more time to second guess. We each stepped into the ocean and immediately descended to escape the waves on the surface.

The two women angled down and away, so I followed. Right away I could tell they were like a pair of fish, effortlessly gliding through the greenish-blue water. They made long, smooth sweeps with their legs and kept every other part of their bodies and gear tucked in and streamlined. I cleared my ears as we descended, and quickly realized the visibility was poor. This was my first time in the Cayman Islands, but they were famous for their legendary underwater clarity. Most days were over a hundred feet of lateral vis across the reef. Not today. The brackish water from the rain mixing with the saltwater had clouded the ocean, and we finally picked up the reef at sixty feet down. It was thirty feet below us. The water steals most of the visible light spectrum at this depth and the colorful reef appeared more like a duotone of blue and green. I saw the drop-off to our right and felt the pull of the current heading south, exactly as AJ had predicted.

She positioned herself near the wall and indicated for me to space myself between her and Nora, who took up position thirty feet over the reef. We began to drift and scan the reef below us. It would be hard to miss something the size of the sailboat, but we were looking for anything that gave us a clue. Anything man-made that suggested a wreck occurred. I was glad it was AJ looking over the wall, I'd be giving myself fits wondering if Grace was down there. Alone in the pitch-black depths.

Fish flitted this way and that around us and occasionally one of us paused to take a second look at something that caught our eye. So far, everything we'd seen had been natural; an odd-shaped coral or sponge. We'd been drifting for a while and I was sure we'd covered the area we had mapped out on the chart. I looked over at AJ and she tapped her dive computer, asking me my tank pressure. I flashed back one finger, then three fingers, indicating I had 1,300 psi of the 3,000 psi I'd started with. She pointed her thumb toward the surface, letting me know we were heading up. We slowly ascended together and spent three minutes at fifteen feet, a safety protocol to rid our bodies of some of the nitrogen and allow our bodies to reacclimatize to the lower surrounding pressure. All the while we were still drifting with the current. I was glad I could see the boat above us, diligently following our bubbles.

I had my doubts about this group, but they seemed incredibly competent, and Nora and AJ barely exchanged a glance and they seemed to know what the other was thinking. I breathed a sigh of relief as we hung, drifting at the will of the ocean. We hadn't found a sailboat. I knew this only ruled out the top of the wall, and it could be lying at the bottom, well out of our view, but something told me it wasn't.

Getting back up the ladder was the hardest part of the dive, as the aluminum frame swung violently in the swells, but once we clambered back aboard with the first mate Thomas's help, I plopped down on a bench and wondered what to do next. I guessed that we'd wait on the sonar to arrive from the States, which would be an agonizing few days from now.

"Take us a hundred meters past where you dropped us, Reg," AJ said to the big fellow. "We'll go in again and cover the first bit. We drifted over it on descent."

Reg nodded and headed back up the ladder to the flybridge.

Apparently, that's what we would do next.

4

It was a bit embarrassing. I knew they both had a lot less body mass than me, but I was relaxed on the dive and I'd let the drift take me. I thought I'd done pretty good on my gas consumption. We were looking at our computers to see how long we needed to sit out before making a second dive, and I saw they both used a fraction of what I sucked down. These women had gills, for Pete's sake.

"We were only in for ten or fifteen minutes, so thirty minutes topside and we'll be fine," AJ assured me. "I just want to cover the north end of our marked area."

By this point, I trusted her completely. I could tell they were all nervous to talk with me, probably unsure what to say to a man who was searching the seafloor for his wife. The police boat stayed clear of us so they didn't have to keep repositioning. They had tied to a mooring buoy farther north and Reg noticed me looking that way.

"Those are all dive site buoys," he said in a London accent, pronouncing buoys like boys. "The Department of Environment sets them and rotates them as needed to rest different parts of the reef." He pointed along the section of ocean where we were floating, "There's nothing along this stretch to moor to."

"How bad was the storm last night?" I asked, as he'd decided to chat with me.

"A lot of rain, some decent wind," he said, scratching his beard. "Not real bad though. We took our boats around to the North Sound overnight. Brought them back west earlier today."

"Capsizing boat type storm?" I asked and searched his face, trying to read whether he was shooting me straight or sugarcoating his answer.

"You can capsize a boat in most any seas if you do enough things wrong," he answered. "But if your missus knew what she was doing, and the motor kept running, no. It wasn't that bad."

I nodded in appreciation, and he nodded back. I liked this guy after all. He wasn't questioning Grace's ability; he was stating a fact.

"All right, gear up," AJ announced. "Let's get back in."

I switched my tank to a fresh one, and neither of them needed to, so they waited on me. I felt like a lame-ass newbie. Reg put us in the new spot, north of where we were, and once he signaled, the three of us took a giant stride off the stern.

More confident this time, I kicked hard for the bottom, clearing my ears, and equalizing my mask as I went. We quickly lined up and began our second search with the current drifting us just as before. The reef looked the same as the first dive, with a wide band of coral at the top of the sloping wall and small fingers extending to the sand flats on our left.

We'd been going less than a minute when I heard a clank, clank, clank. AJ was signaling with a stainless-steel carabiner against her tank. Nora and I swam over, and right away I noticed how hard it was to stay in one spot. We had drifted the entire time, but now to maintain position against the current took considerable effort. AJ pointed down the sloping wall and I looked over the edge. I had no idea what she was pointing at, but there was no sailboat, to my relief.

AJ and Nora flashed a few hand signals and apparently a plan had been made, as I watched AJ kick head-down toward the depths. Nora tapped my arm and indicated with her hand that I should stay here. No shit, Ice Queen, I wasn't going down there. I was busy swimming my ass off against the current which didn't seem to affect Nora in the least bit. She softly finned next to me as I tried to watch what AJ was up to. I still couldn't see what she went after. She stopped at what I guessed was 130-feet or so, right at the edge of our visibility, and pulled something from the steeply sloped coral-covered wall.

I saw her glance at her dive computer, and I was getting anxious myself. A second dive to that depth was not the plan and she had to be pushing deco. I was breathing heavily and sucking down gas just to stay put at a hundred feet, watching my nitrogen load build and my own time until deco dropping. AJ finally gathered up whatever treasure she found and was gliding back toward us. When she reached the top of the wall she didn't even pause, and Nora tugged my arm to follow. We went straight up, careful not to ascend too fast and risk the bends, but we weren't dawdling either. The current was our taxi once more, like an underwater conveyor.

AJ leveled off at thirty feet and tapped her computer,

looking at me. I signaled I had 1,600 psi. I'd been a lot better than that until I had to swim against the current like an Olympian. AJ and Nora exchanged a few nods and a couple of hand signals. I'd rather not know how little gas they'd used; I felt inferior enough already. But I did want to know what AJ went after and I tapped her arm where she had whatever it was cradled out of view.

She held up a canister with an aerial sticking out of the top. I gasped into my regulator. It was an EPIRB, but not just any EPIRB. It was the model we purchased for Grace to take with her to the BVI. Attached to the base was a short length of line. AJ held up the other end, where a three-pound dive weight was tied.

We completed our safety stops at 30-feet and 15-feet, then fought the flying ladder to get back on the boat. I was still in shock and trying to process. I dropped my gear in the rack and AJ handed me the EPIRB. They were individually serialized so it would be easy to check if it was a match, but I already knew it was. The weight tied to the base and three holes drilled in the floating base section also left no doubt it was intended for the bottom of the ocean. Water poured from the holes as I examined the canister.

"Is there any way this was a decoy?" AJ asked me.

I went blank. That thought hadn't occurred to me, "You mean, could another boat have brought this here and sunk it on purpose?"

"Right," she clarified. "To throw you off track and have you looking in the wrong place."

"If they turned it on, let it send a good signal," Reg weighed in, "then tossed it over what they thought was the deep, they probably reckoned we'd be weeks searching at eight hundred feet or more."

"Storm caught it just right and plonked it on the side of the wall," AJ said. "Bloody lucky really."

"How deep were you?" I asked, realizing the lengths she'd gone to retrieve something I couldn't even see. "How did you stay out of deco?"

"One hundred twenty-nine feet, and I didn't," she grinned back.

"You were in deco?" I asked to be sure. It was a golden rule of recreational diving to never go over the no-decompression limit. Technical divers did it all the time and had stage decompression stops on mixed gases to get out of it. There was risk involved.

"Just a bit," she said, shrugging her shoulders like it was no big deal. "I managed it with the safety stops. Bit close on gas though, probably should have switched tanks after all."

Frankly, I was a little overwhelmed. These people didn't even know me, or my wife, and they came straight out at a moment's notice to go the extra mile and help out. I felt like shit for thinking the detective was rounding up a bunch of yahoos. I was also totally confused over what to think about Grace and our sailboat. I couldn't come up with a single reason why anyone would tie a weight to an emergency signal device and throw it off a sinking boat. That was the good news; I was confident the sailboat wasn't at the bottom of this particular seafloor. But I was no clearer on where it might be or why it was seemingly wandering around the Caribbean.

Maybe they were right, perhaps this was set up as a diversion. Or maybe the EPIRB was tossed from our sailboat for a reason I couldn't fathom.

I pictured the central Caribbean in my mind and imagined a line from the top of Haiti to Grand Cayman, passing between Cuba and Jamaica. From Grand Cayman, sweeping north around the west end of Cuba was the old sailing route of the Spanish fleets carrying treasure back from the New World. They would cut east up the Straits of Florida, past the Keys on their way back to Europe. They used the longer route because of the trade winds and the Gulf Stream currents. A modern sailboat could run our planned route up the leeward island chain in far less time. She had no reason to take the long way home.

West of Cayman was a lot of empty ocean until Mexico and the Yucatán peninsula. Grace had even less reason to go to Mexico. But if I carried my imaginary line across the map in my head, that would be the destination.

Thomas gave me a towel and I slipped out of the wetsuit they'd loaned me. I was digging my shirt from my backpack when my cell phone rang. My heart skipped every time the damn thing rang as I knew what could be on the end of the call. It wasn't happening until I knew it was. Denial was safe harbor. I took a deep breath and answered the phone.

"Nathan Fitzgerald?" came a stern voice I didn't recognize.

"Yes," I replied, half expecting an offer to extend the warranty on my car.

"This is Special Agent Foster with the FBI. I've been assigned to your case."

"My case?" This struck me as odd. I wasn't missing. "Don't you mean my wife Grace's case?"

"One and the same, sir," he responded flatly. "Where are you currently, Mr. Fitzgerald?"

I didn't want to be uncooperative, but I didn't really know who I was talking to and between the ocean noise on my end and all kinds of background chatter on his, it was hard to hear.

"How do I know you're an FBI agent?"

That had everyone on the boat looking my way.

"Across this phone line you have no way of being sure, sir," he said calmly. "But I assure you, I am who I say I am."

And a bad guy would never stoop so low as to say that. He ought to know where I am, hell, if Grace's boss knew where I was going, it shouldn't be hard for the Federal Bureau of Investigation to know. I was about to hang up.

"I spoke with Detective Whittaker earlier today, is he with you?"

"He's on another boat. We're on the water," I replied. Maybe he was legit, and I was about to hang up on the FBI. I was so out of my depth.

"Have you been able…" he said some more stuff, but all I heard was an announcement in the background.

"You'll have to say that again, it's really noisy wherever you are," I told him.

"Final call, we're boarding all groups to Cozumel, Mexico," Damn, he was at an airport, I realized. No wonder it was noisy, "Have you found anything?" he repeated.

"We found the EPIRB," I told him. "I'm sure it's from our sailboat, but no wreckage."

Foster paused for a moment, "Go home, Mr. Fitzgerald, let us do our job. I promise we're looking very hard for your wife. I have to go, but I'll call you again, soon."

The line went dead.

"That was the FBI?" Nora asked, a hint of surprise in her deadpan expression.

"I think so," I said, hesitantly. "He said he was."

"Don't they shoot you for impersonating an FBI agent?"

AJ quipped. "Or banish you to some shit hole like…" she looked at Reg, "I was gonna say Barnsley, but he won't know where Barnsley is. What's a really shit town in America?"

"How the hell do I know," Reg replied. "You lived there for three years."

I was mesmerized for a moment by their banter back and forth. "Mendota, California."

"Really?" Thomas chimed in. "I thought California was fine beaches and all?"

"Mendota, California, was voted the worst place to live in America," I said, and couldn't believe I knew this. I wasn't even sure how I knew this, but everyone seemed satisfied that we'd resolved the issue.

"So, what now?" AJ asked and looked at me.

"The FBI guy wants me to go home," I admitted.

"Where do you want to go?" Nora and AJ asked at the same time.

I thought for a few moments. This was getting more and more bizarre, but I couldn't stop now. "I think I need to go to Cozumel. I believe the FBI guy is heading there, and if the sailboat kept going west, it's where they'd hit land."

Nora nodded, which I took as approval.

"Ooh," AJ grinned, "I have someone you have to meet in Cozumel."

"Are they as cool as you guys?"

AJ laughed, "You have no idea."

PART II

5

By the time I descended the boarding stairs to the apron at Cozumel International Airport, the sun had set and the western sky was rapidly losing its orange glow. Nevertheless, the tarmac under my feet still radiated heat, and the humidity was just beginning to dissipate in the evening breeze.

The previous afternoon's dives had been deep enough that the early morning flight out of Grand Cayman might have been risky, so I'd opted for a later flight. I was blessed with a minor miracle, scoring a last-minute window seat, and managing to catch some much-needed sleep during the second leg from Miami. There were no direct flights between Cozumel and Grand Cayman, a fact that had surprised me, given their proximity. I guess people don't often fly from paradise to paradise.

Mine was one of the last flights in and I sped through customs, reaching the curbside in short order. Offers of "Taxi!" assailed my ears from all directions, but my eyes were drawn to a peculiar automobile that sat by the curb at the back of a line of red-striped, white cabs.

Bright yellow and boxy, the vehicle looked like the unholy union of an open-topped Jeep and a World War II German staff car. Several descriptive words came to mind, "rust-bucket" being at the forefront. A man and woman stood beside the automotive oddity, the pair as striking as their car.

The man looked to be in his late twenties or early thirties and was very tall—taller than my six feet by a number of inches. He wore cargo shorts and sandals beneath a faded dive shirt, with a logo for "Bubble Chasers Diving" emblazoned on it. An unruly mop of sun-frosted brown hair topped a tanned face, and his frame was long and lanky. That being said, from what I could see of his bare arms and legs, that skinny physique was sculpted in ropy muscle.

His companion was on the other end of the scale, her blond head at the level of the man's chest, a petite and curvy figure beneath her striped tank top and shorts. Her lightly tanned legs descended to a pair of bright-green tennis shoes. Even though the sun's glow was nearly gone, she sported an enormous pair of lime-green sunglasses, and what I could see of her face would be described by any casual observer as drop-dead beautiful. She looked to be late twenties, though the pigtails she'd braided her golden hair into gave her a more youthful quality.

The tall man looked my way before leaning down and saying something to the blonde. Her face suddenly lit up with a megawatt smile as she aimed her shades toward me and whipped a homemade sign from behind her back. It read "Nathan." She flipped it. "Fitzgerald" was on the back.

She spun the sign in a continuous motion, nodding knowingly as she looked at me.

If my wife's life didn't hang in the balance, I might have laughed. I raised a hand in greeting, hefting my backpack and duffel as I made my way over to the pair, reminding myself of my hasty and inaccurate judgment of the folks in Grand Cayman. "I'm guessing you're my ride?" I asked.

"Boone Fischer," the man said, extending a hand which I shook. "And this—"

"Emily Durand," the young woman interrupted, tucking her giant sunglasses into the neckline of her tank top. "Welcome to Coz." She handed me the sign. "Here. Little souvenir, yeah?"

Emily spoke with a blue-collar English accent—not exactly cartoon Cockney, but definitely not something you'd hear in Buckingham Palace.

"So… Nathan Fitzgerald… do I call you Nate, or do I call you Fitz? Or how about Gerald? Jerry?"

I smiled. "Nathan's fine." I started to tuck the cardboard sign under my arm, but Boone reached out to take it, and tossed it into the car.

"Don't worry, she'll calm down in a bit."

"Not in your Volkswagen Thing I won't," Em replied. "Pins 'n' needles the whole way. Your life insurance paid up, Nathaniel?"

I managed another smile. She was very charming, but I was exhausted; and the mention of life insurance—though clearly in jest—sent my mind to a dark place. Grace and I had recently discussed getting life insurance policies, but we'd never gotten around to it.

Boone seemed to pick up on my shift in mood. "Let's get on the road, Nathan, and you can tell us how we can help.

AJ over in Grand Cayman gave us the lowdown, but maybe you can fill in a few things." He took my bags and set them in the backseat beside a brown dog I'd just now noticed, the harness across its chest strapped to a seatbelt. Of medium size, the short-haired pooch had ears that turned down at the tips. His brown eyes regarded me intently, and a six-inch tail furiously thumped the surface of the backseat.

"This here's Brixton," Em said. "Brix for short. An absolute lick-monster, but he's a pussycat. Well… not literally, of course. Brix is a Belizean potlicker… which is a fancy term for mutt."

I laughed. "Grace and I have a fur-buddy ourselves. Bogey. Yellow lab."

"Ew!" Emily grimaced, putting a finger up to her nose. "Like a bogey?"

I had no idea what she meant.

"A bogey is a booger in the UK," Boone translated for me.

"Oh." I shook my head, still shaking off the cobwebs of the flight. "No. Bogey is a golf term for one over par."

"That's much more respectable." Em replied, apparently happy with the explanation, "Sit up front with Boone, you'll be able to hear better. The engine's in the back on this old banger and it's inhabited by a death-metal hard rock band. We woulda picked you up in my VW Bug, but irony of ironies, it's the one in the shop."

"You get a meal on the plane?" Boone inquired, as we settled into the threadbare seats.

"I'm okay," I said.

"That sounds like a no." He turned the key in the ignition and the engine on the 1970s relic burbled into some semblance of life. "We'll get some eats."

"La Choza?" Em asked from beside my ear, startling me. She was sitting on the edge of the backseat, leaning forward between us.

"Sounds like a plan," Boone replied, wrenching the Thing into gear, and heading for the airport exit.

"Really, I'm good," I said. "I don't want to put you out. And you've probably already eaten."

"That won't stop Boone," Em said. "And I'll get a slice of the avocado pie!"

"Actually, Nathan… La Choza's a good place to talk." Boone took a right at the traffic circle just outside the airport. "It's a restaurant two streets back from the main drag, so the cruise ship hordes don't tend to find it. The locals eat there and it's pretty chill."

Leaving the airport, I looked around at the scenery. In some respects, Cozumel looked a lot like Grand Cayman: a decidedly flat landscape populated with low tropical shrubs and palm trees, the occasional flamboyant tree breaking up the wall of green with splashes of vibrant red.

After a moment, we took a left into the town, the streets lined with squat houses, many painted in bright colors. Low concrete walls were between many of the properties, their painted surfaces decorated with graffiti and the occasional advertisement.

"We'll be there in a sec," Boone said.

"Okay. Thanks. So… from what AJ told me, you two have a dive op?"

"We do indeed," Boone said. "Bubble Chasers Diving. Most of the diving in Cozumel is drift diving. The currents are strong, so the divers just go with the flow and the dive boats 'chase' the bubbles and pick them up when they surface."

"I came up with the name," Emily chimed in. "And the name of our boat."

I turned my head, finding her smiling face. "Which is?"

"*Lunasea*," she said. "You'll get it when you see it. I liked my other one better, though."

I raised my eyebrows expectantly.

"Quit Looking at My Stern," Boone supplied, the ghost of a smirk on his lips. "I vetoed that one. Too much paint."

I laughed, shaking my head. "That's good."

"I know, it's ace, innit? I suggested Quit Looking at My Aft as an alternative, but 'Joy Vacuum' here wouldn't go for that one, either."

Boone's face cracked at that. He came across as a pretty stoic guy, but it was clear this petite British spitfire tickled what little funny bone he had. He tossed a glance my way. "This new sailboat of yours AJ told us about... did you rename her yet?"

"No... she's still got the name she had when we bought her. *Anegada Da Vida*. Yeah, I know... corny. Play on words between that rock song and one of the islands in the BVI. We were going to change it but didn't want to do that without a proper naming ceremony. Heard it was bad luck." I swallowed hard and gave a rueful laugh. "Though, I dunno... maybe we shoulda..."

"Nathan." Boone slowed as he neared a turn and held my eyes for a moment. "If your wife's coming to Coz, we'll find her."

I nodded, not trusting my voice to reply. As we turned, I dug my cell phone out of my pocket. "Hey, does this restaurant have Wi-Fi?"

"Yeah," Boone said. "Annnnnnd... here it is." He turned onto a narrow street and pulled over to the curb.

"C'mon, Brix! Time for a little under-table snooze!" Emily unlatched the dog from the seatbelt. "Oh, Nate... grab your bags. Boone's trunk doesn't lock anymore, fancy that, so we better bring them in."

Seated in a back corner of La Choza with a few local dishes in front of us, I laid everything out to the two divemasters. Boone listened quietly and Emily's boisterous manner sobered considerably. When I finished summing up, I took a sip of my cerveza. "I think that's it," I said after a moment.

"The EPIRB," Emily began. "You're sure that was sabotage?"

"Holes drilled in it and added weight... yeah, someone wanted it to sink to the bottom."

"And based on where they tossed it overboard," Boone mused, "whoever dropped it wanted it to go deep. To make you think the sailboat sank there."

"Right."

"But there's nothing saying that beacon was on the sailboat at the time it was dropped," Boone pointed out. "It could've been dropped from a helicopter or a fishing boat. Or maybe it *was* on the sailboat when it was ditched... but it's possible your wife wasn't aboard."

"Boone..." Emily muttered in a warning tone. "Touch of optimism, yeah?"

I swallowed. I had considered these possibilities. And if pirates had taken the Island Packet, they might have... *No, don't go there.*

"It feels like misdirection," Boone mused. He looked up and held my eyes. "But sometimes you gotta go with your gut, and I've got a feeling you think it's on its way here."

I thought about the boarding call for Cozumel I'd overheard on the phone call with Agent Foster. *Well… the guy who* said *he was an FBI agent*, my mind amended.

"Yes," I said with conviction. "I realize there are other possibilities, but it's a straight line across to Cozumel, and something tells me she's on her way here."

Boone nodded. "Good enough for me. What's the top speed on your sailboat, any idea?"

"Well, I've never been on it, but I remember the sellers said it had a cruising speed of six knots on engine power. Top speed wasn't much higher. But it's got sails, of course."

"And AJ said Grand had quite a blow the night before," Em mused. "Probably could do the whole passage at seven knots."

Boone was futzing on his phone. "An Island Packet at cruising speed can manage 500 nautical miles without refueling. But it's about 325 from there to here, and I'm betting they didn't refuel in Grand Cayman with that weather system. If it were me and I hadn't refueled since—I dunno, Jamaica? —I wouldn't push the speed. Em, you're the goddess of skippering… thoughts?"

"Let's split the difference. Six and a half knots. With help from the sails, easy peasy. What time did the beacon warning happen?"

"Yesterday, about seven a.m."

"So… 325 nautical miles at six and a half knots… leaving Grand seven a.m. yesterday… I'm rubbish at maths. Boone?"

"On it." Under Boone's pen, a paper napkin gave its life for the cause. "Fifty hours, about."

"So… nine a.m. tomorrow morning," I said.

"Okay…" Boone's eyes went distant for a few seconds before snapping back into focus. "All right, here's what we're gonna do. I'll call our co-owner, Ricardo, and have him reach out to his uncle with the Marine Park. He'll pass the word to the park staff and they can also ask the Mexican Navy to keep an eye out. We saw one of their patrol boats out-and-about when we were coming in from the afternoon dive yesterday. But that's just a start. Em, feel like making some calls to the tribe?"

Emily smiled, slipping her phone from a pocket in her white shorts. "On it. Nathan, we've got our own dive op, yeah? But half our business is subbing ourselves out to the other ops on the island. Sometimes a boat breaks down or they overbook. Anyhoo, we can get a lot more eyeballs looking for your wife. Thirty-eight-foot Island Packet, yeah? Name of *Anegada Da Vida*. Hey, got any pics?"

"Oh, yeah, good idea." I opened my phone—I had logged into the restaurant's Wi-Fi the moment we sat down in the hopes some message from my wife had come in during my flight. No such luck. And nothing new from CyberWard or the FBI. Opening the mail app, I scrolled back in time, looking for the first conversations Grace and I had had with the original owners. "I've got a photo in one of these emails... I'll send it to you once I find it."

Boone had swiped Emily's napkin and was scribbling on it. "Em, whattaya think? Dive Paradise, Aqua Safari, Scuba Life, Cozumel Marine World, Scuba Tony... hit them up first and have them spread the word?"

"Don't forget Jorge at Marino Mundo. He'll do anything for me, Boone," Em teased.

"Your dance club partner in crime, how could I forget," Boone said with a grin as he finished scribbling and slid the napkin to Emily.

"Here's the photo," I said.

Boone continued his napkin crime spree, stealing mine to scribble a pair of numbers on it before handing it back. "Just WhatsApp it to us and we'll get this in everyone's hands."

The waiter came by and inquired about dessert. Em thanked him but asked for the check.

"Thought you were going to get some avocado pie," I remarked.

"No time for sweets, Nate! We've got a lot of calls to make."

6

The enticing smell of coffee woke me. Glancing toward the glass doors to the balcony, I could see it was still pitch black. My phone said it was five a.m., and the burbling sound of a coffee pot told me someone else was up. I swung my feet to the cool tile floor of the condominium's living room. I'd expected a sleepless night—not from any lack of comfort from the futon I was occupying, but from the anxiety chattering away in my skull. But I'd been running on adrenaline since I'd gotten the EPIRB notification and exhaustion had won out. I rose and padded to the balcony. Sliding the door open, I stepped from the air conditioning into the humid tropical air, locking my eyes on the waters of the Cozumel Channel, its surface illuminated only by starlight. We were quite some distance south of the main town of San Miguel, and the early morning sounds consisted of little more than insects and surf.

Grace… I'll see you today, God willing.

"Oh, you're up." Emily poked her head out of the living room. She was sporting an XLT T-shirt, likely one of

Boone's, the shirt advertising Belikin: The Beer of Belize. "Hope we didn't wake you."

"No. Just got up."

"Good. Boone wants to get an early start. I'll pour you a cuppa. Coffee, that is. How d'you take it?"

"Black. Thanks."

"*De nada.*" She vanished into the gloom of the condo, her bare feet slapping their way across the tile.

I looked back out to sea, my hands gripping the balcony railing, wringing it.

"We'll find her," Boone said from beside me.

I jumped. I hadn't even heard him join me. "I hope so."

He took a sip of his coffee. "By nine a.m., we'll have a big net of eyeballs out there. But I figured we should get going early—head down to the marina where the *Lunasea* is berthed. Make sure the *Anegada Da Vida* didn't haul ass and dock somewhere already. There's only three marinas where you could refuel, and I've got a couple buds who will check the other two."

"Thank you for doing all this," I said.

"Hey, if it were Em out there... I wouldn't rest until I found her."

"And if it were Boone out there," Emily said from the doorway, "I'd do the same. I've saved his arse as often as he's saved mine."

Boone smiled over the rim of his cup. "She keeps score."

"Somebody has to." Em handed me a cup of joe. "I've got a thermos for the road. Pound that coffee down and get dressed, Nate. Let's go find Grace."

The sun was cresting the low vegetation that spanned the interior of Cozumel as the *Lunasea* made its way out of the Marina Fonatur. A thorough search of the slips had yielded nothing, and Boone had received texts from his contacts at the other two marinas indicating they'd had no luck either. I stood atop the flybridge, eyes scanning every boat I could see in the early dawn light.

Emily Durand took the helm, navigating her way out of the entrance with effortless nudges of the wheel and throttle. Below, Bubble Chasers' co-owner, a local named Ricardo Pérez, secured a number of scuba tanks. I watched as he began to attach a set of scuba gear to one of them.

"We were scheduled to do a lionfish cull this morning," Boone said as he came up the ladder and joined me atop the flybridge. "Since we've got the gear, I asked Ric to assemble a couple rigs."

"Sorry if I canceled a charter," I said.

"Nah, it was just us. We try to do one every week or so."

"The waters around Key Largo are lousy with those things."

"Yeah, everywhere in the Caribbean has them now. Since they're a Pacific species and invasive, few predators around here know how to eat them… except us. They make fantastic fish tacos."

"The Key Largo Conch House serves them sometimes," I said.

"Good," Boone said firmly. "We'll eat those bastards out of the Western Hemisphere. Em and I teach a course, and graduates can join us on our culls."

"North or south?" Emily called back as we neared the drop-off to the channel. The sun was largely behind us, but Emily was already sporting those enormous green sunglasses.

"Let's start north," Boone said, joining her at the wheel.

"I want to be sure we sweep the approach to those marinas in case she's already here on the lee side."

"Right-o," Em said, spinning the wheel to starboard. "And Jorge's going out early this morning to beat the other ops to the Devil's Throat, so he'll be near the southern tip by nine."

We motored north, the dive boat picking up speed over the deeper waters of the Cozumel Channel. To my right, enormous piers jutted out from shore, several cruise ships already at dock. We seemed to be moving at a fair clip and the ride got bouncy at times. Boone had a small pair of binoculars to his eyes and ended up smacking himself on the bridge of his nose.

"Easy there, Fast and Furious."

"Sorry!" Em called out, throttling back.

Boone looked back at me. "The *Lunasea* has some extra juice under the hood, but the hull's not exactly designed for going flat out if there's any chop."

"What kind of boat is this?" I asked.

"Delta Canaveral… but with some custom adjustments. She used to belong to drug runners. Long story."

"I'd love to hear it someday…" I said, my voice trailing off as I stared out across the water, watching for approaching boats.

"Hey, Nathan, I was wondering…" Boone looked uncomfortable. "How come you're not on board with Grace?"

I sighed. "Dumb luck. I needed an emergency crown. Broke a tooth on an unpitted date."

Emily visibly winced. "Ooh… sorry, mate."

"I don't think I've ever eaten a date," Boone mused absently.

Emily burst into uncontrollable laughter, its sound so infectious I couldn't help but grin. She managed to catch her breath. "Your dates must have been so disappointed," she gasped. "Oh, my, Boone, you've got to watch your phrasing."

I chuckled, watching as Boone caught on and shook his head with a smile. "Careful what you say around Chuckles McGee here." His smile slipped a bit. "So that's why you hired someone to sail it with her. What do you know about this guy?"

"Not much… but he came highly recommended from someone my wife met in the British Virgin Islands. Name's Brandon."

Just then, Emily's cell phone rang from her back pocket. One hand still on the wheel, she reached back and slid it out to look at the screen. "It's Jorge. Boone, take the wheel, yeah?" She stepped aside and answered. "*Hola*, Jorge!" Her always-smiling face took on a look of deep concentration and she plugged her free ear with a finger. "Say again?" She listened intently. "Right, we're on our way!" Pocketing the phone, she hip-checked Boone aside and retook the wheel. "Budge up, I've got it. Hang on, Nathan!" Spinning the wheel to port, she pushed the throttle to the stops. From below, I heard Ricardo yelp at the unexpected change in direction.

"Sorry, Ricardo!" Em called out.

"What did the man on the phone say?" I shouted, gripping the flybridge rail.

"He said he's spotted your boat! And it's not alone!"

7

The *Lunasea* tore through the deeper indigo waters of the channel as we raced south. Emily was forced to throttle back several times, the shape of the dive boat's hull making for a rough ride. Far astern, several dive boats were just making their own way south, headed for the more popular dive sites.

"The Island Packet's all the way down south, almost to Maracaibo!" Emily yelled back over her shoulder. "Marina Mundo was going to dive the Devil's Throat, but Jorge spotted your sailboat as he neared Punta Sur. He said there's some kind of Cigarette boat alongside."

"Don't see those out here too often," Boone pointed out.

Em nodded, teeth clamping her plump lower lip in concentration as she navigated the waves. "He didn't recognize it. No name or home port on it."

Being from Florida, I knew all about the go-fast boats, known colloquially as "Cigarette boats." These sleek, low-slung boats were often associated with smuggling; their high speeds allowed them to outrun most Coast Guard boats and their close-to-the-water height made them hard to spot on radar until you were close.

"Did he see anyone aboard the *Anegada Da Vida*?" I asked above the roar of the engine, a note of desperation in my voice.

Emily looked back at me, her sunglasses making her eyes unreadable. "He didn't say."

I sat down on the deck of the flybridge and tore into my backpack, finding the sat phone and scrolling through the contacts. There were only three, this being a new purchase, and I stabbed Grace's number. Straight to voicemail. Dammit.

"How far is it?" I shouted.

Boone glanced to port. "That's our condo right there. From here, it's ten miles to the southern tip… roughly eight and a half nautical miles. Em's managing about thirty knots. Should be on site in a little over fifteen minutes."

I stuffed my phone back into my pack and rose, eyes straining toward the south. After a few minutes, Emily's phone rang again and Boone pickpocketed it from her shorts.

"Is it Jorge?" she asked, eyes still on the horizon.

"Yeah. Keep doing what you're doing… you're the better skipper."

"Won't get any argument from me," she replied with a grin.

"Jorge, *mi amigo!* It's Boone. We're about fifteen minutes out." He listened intently, his eyes going wide. "Shit." He shoved Em's phone back in her pocket and went toward the stern side of the flybridge. "Ricardo! Get low and hang on! You too, Nathan! Em… screw the bumps, floor it!" He headed to starboard, looking out across the channel, the Mexican mainland just visible on the horizon.

"What's happening?" I yelled, as Emily once more pushed the throttle to the max and the boat banged against the waves.

"The *Anegada* is sinking!" Boone shouted, dropping to his knees, and pulling his small binoculars from his cargo shorts. "Jorge said there was a loud boom and then the Cigarette boat headed north… there!"

I raised my head and could see a long-hulled shape tearing across the waves, a silvery bow wave gleaming in the tropical sun, the shining spray occasionally interrupted when the sleek boat left the surface of the water and knifed through the air before smacking back down into the sea. Even at this distance—nearly a mile, I guessed—you could hear the boat's impact on the waves and its roaring engine. The boat's cockpit area was sunken and it was difficult to make out the occupants. As it flashed by, the vessel banked to port, heading across the Cozumel Channel.

"Jeez, that thing has six outboards!" Boone called out.

I turned to the lanky divemaster, who was doing his best to track the fast-moving boat with his binoculars. "Can you see her? Can you see Grace?"

Boone cursed under his breath as a brutal bounce jerked the binos clear of his eyes. "Em," he screamed, "slow down a sec!" When the bouncing abruptly abated, he jammed the binoculars back into place. "Hard to make anything out. I can see two occupants… both look male, but I can't be sure. The way the cockpit well is designed, I can only make out the tops of their heads."

"Then she might be on the sailboat," I shouted.

Boone lowered the binos. "Em! Crank it!" The dive

boat's engine roared again and I watched as the Cigarette's cascading wake receded into the distance. Boone reached beside Emily and flipped the marine radio to Channel 16. A Mexican-accented voice crackled to life. The message was delivered in rapid-fire Spanish before the speaker switched to English.

Mayday, mayday, mayday! This is Barco Rapido of Marino Mundo Diving off Punta Sur. A sailboat is sinking near dive site Maracaibo. I have divers in the water and cannot assist. Over.

Lunasea powered past a dive boat moored near the drop-off to the channel. A man waved and pointed emphatically to the south.

"That's Jorge," Boone called out. "The sailboat should be visible from here…"

"I see it!" Emily made an adjustment to the wheel, aiming her bow toward a white shape about a mile ahead. The seas were rougher than up north, ocean swells frothing to white caps here and there.

I scrambled forward, my heart rising into my throat as the object came into focus. The *Anegada Da Vida* was down at the stern, her deck awash, the mast tipping back at a forty-five-degree angle. Water bubbled and frothed at its sides, probably from displaced air. Lightweight objects, including empty life vests, floated free of the boat.

"Oh God… Grace!"

"Shit… it's going down too fast," Boone rasped, binoculars locked on the wreckage. "Em, bring us alongside! The current's going to propel it as it goes down, so keep us a little north of it." With that, he grabbed the flybridge ladder and scrambled down. "Ricardo! Grab the lifebuoy!"

I followed, practically leaping down the ladder after him. Boone was stripping off his shirt, revealing a lean, wiry physique. Going further, he lost the cargo shorts, before tearing into a gear bag and retrieving a mask and weight belt with a single three-pounder on it.

"What are you doing?" I gasped, stepping to the gunwale, and looking across the starboard bow toward the rapidly sinking boat.

"I'm going in. I didn't see anyone in the water and she might be trapped inside." He pulled on booties and fins.

"Then I'm going, too!"

"No, you're not. Down here at the tip, the ocean swells are bad and currents are unpredictable. I'm a skilled freediver and I'll have my hands full as it is. Stay here." With that, he planted his long arms and raised himself from the bench onto the gunwale, looking back over his shoulder. "Em! Closer!" His eyes on the Island Packet, Boone sucked in a deep breath, paused, then slowly exhaled for a surprisingly long time.

The *Lunasea* pitched and rolled and her engine pulsed as Emily fought to navigate the swells as she came alongside the *Anegada Da Vida*. "It's almost under!" I cried out, watching as the boat slipped further beneath the waves, only her bow and the top of the mast above the surface.

Boone didn't reply, his chest expanding again, clearly defined ribs pressing against his tanned skin. Wordlessly, he rolled backwards into the water.

Without a second thought, I emptied my pockets onto the camera table mounted in the center of the deck and dropped onto the bench in front of one of the sets of scuba gear, twisting around to open the tank's valve. With practiced movements, I slid into the BCD and felt the sides. Good. This one had integrated weights in pouches. Without those, I'd bob on the surface like a cork. I spared a quick glance at the pressure gauge.

Plenty, I thought.

"*Qué?* What are you doing?" Ricardo shouted, as he came back around from the bow, a bright orange-and-white life preserver hoop in hand.

"I'm a rescue diver back in Florida," I lied, figuring that if it worked with AJ back on Grand Cayman, it would work now. "And I'm not just going to sit here while my wife's boat sinks!"

Ricardo dropped the lifebuoy, scrambling for his own gear bag. "Then you'll probably want a mask and fins, *si*?" He handed me a mask as I kicked off my deck shoes. Crouching, Ricardo slid a pair of fins onto my bare feet, cinching the straps tight. "I'm sorry, but my boots won't fit you."

I'd never used fins without boots, so I figured I'd be in for some serious blisters; but in the grand scheme of things, it was a trivial concern.

"We're off the reef here… the channel drops to 400 meters, so watch your depth!" Ricardo helped me onto the gunwale. "I see a lot of line in the water, and it looks like some of the sails have come loose. Be careful not to entangle yourself."

I nodded as I rammed the regulator's mouthpiece into place, took a test breath, then cupped a hand over my mask and mouthpiece and rolled backwards into the sea.

After a moment of disorientation, I flipped upright and turned toward the Island Packet. The current pulled me to my right, but that same current was exerting itself on the sailboat. Objects continued to float free of the sinking boat and the mainsail had broken loose from its sail ties and was billowing out, obscuring parts of the *Anegada Da Vida* in a ghostly shroud. Boone was nowhere in sight. My eyes were immediately drawn to a jagged hole near the stern, pieces of hull splintered outward around its edges. *What on earth did that?* I kicked hard for the portside of the boat, descending to where I could peer into the cabin portholes.

Coming alongside, I dodged a line that was uncoiling into the water column. It looked like one of the halyards to hoist the sail, and I juked to the side to reach the hull. Looking into a porthole, I saw movement! My adrenaline was already running high, and this pumped it into overdrive. Heart pounding in my ears, I kicked toward the stern, intending to enter the cabin from the companionway.

And that's when the *Anegada Da Vida* broke free of the surface tension. Its descent increased dramatically—the strong, northerly current sent her plunging diagonally. I surged for the companionway and started to enter. Pockets of air were visible near the ceiling, and the entire cabin was shadowy, the gloom increasing as the vessel sank. I heard a loud creak from outside—likely the aluminum mast breaking free. I looked back out to the stern and noticed the water outside darkening in hue, the deck pitching downward as the flooded stern pulled at the stricken vessel. There was a sensation of tumbling. Outside the companionway, the abyss beckoned.

Oh my God… I'm going to die here.

Suddenly, a strong grip clamped onto my upper left arm and I could feel the top of my tank being pulled toward the exit. Boone had come up behind me, from the inside. He must have been the movement I'd seen through the porthole. Boone hadn't been visible when I entered, so I assumed he'd been down in the staterooms. At first, I didn't resist. But then my eyes spotted something familiar floating in the corner of the cabin.

Straining against Boone's grip, I managed to snag a strap on the object. Clutching it tightly, I oriented myself toward the companionway and together we kicked free of the cabin. My brain expected to see the sunlit surface above, but the boat must have tilted down drastically. Looking to my right, one of the sails was now completely unfurled, fluttering up in the whipping current as the heavier boat plunged, and above its gleaming white expanse I could make out the surface.

Boone pulled me hard to the side, getting us clear of the wreck, then held up a flattened hand, indicating we should stop. He made for a bizarre site—nothing but mask, fins, and boxer shorts between him and the deep. I'd heard that freedivers could stay down for a very long time, but he would probably need to surface soon.

Boone looked upward, then grabbed my depth gauge and glanced at it. I saw his eyes widen behind his mask. He reached to my side and took my yellow octopus, the secondary regulator connected to my tank. Placing the octo in his mouth, he again held up his hand, then looked at my BCD and fished around in a side pocket, coming up with an underwater writing slate. *I must've grabbed his gear.*

Boone scrawled on the slate and held it up.

Grace not on board.

My breath hitched in my chest and a relieved sob burst from behind my regulator's mouthpiece. I looked down and watched the *Anegada Da Vida* rapidly sink into the abyss, trailing lines and sails like a plunging jellyfish. Boone's slate appeared in front of my vision once more, with additional words.

We're deep. Ascend slowly. Current strong. Stay with me.

Nodding my understanding, I kicked gently. Looking at my gauges, I could see we were below a hundred feet. Sparing another glance toward my fins, my eyes sought out the sailboat. It was gone, swallowed by the depths.

After an agonizingly slow ascent and a three-minute safety stop, we finally broke the surface. The ocean was rough, and I was relieved to see the *Lunasea* was right there, keeping pace with us just down-current from our position. Far atop the flybridge I could see Emily craning her neck back, shouting something to Ricardo, who waited on the stern swim platform. He shot her a thumbs-up and tossed a trailing line out to us.

I grabbed hold. "Damn, she's good," I gasped, before popping my reg back in my mouth just before an ocean swell smacked me in the face.

"She's the best," Boone called out from beside me, pride in his voice. "And Bubble Chasers is a damn good name. Even in this chop, she was with us the whole time."

In minutes we were aboard and I sank onto a bench slot, exhausted. Boone sat down on the deck, breathing heavily. He pulled off his mask and looked at me. "Are you all right?" he asked.

I thought about my only lead, plunging to the bottom of the Cozumel Channel. "I will be… if I can track down that go-fast boat."

"Emily called it in to the Harbor Master," Ricardo said. "The Mexican Navy may try to locate it, but honestly… it's faster than anything they have here."

"Maybe a helicopter…"

"Maybe," Ricardo said, a note of doubt in his voice. "If they had one at the ready. But it looked like it was going across to Playa del Carmen, and at the speed it was going, they could make the crossing in ten minutes."

"If that's where they were headed, they would've reached there before we even got back aboard," Boone said. Then he abruptly raised his head. "What was it you grabbed when I was trying to get you out?"

I suddenly realized I still had a death grip on the strap. I held the object up. "My wife's laptop bag. Minus the laptop."

8

Once we were back in the shallows, Emily idled the boat and came down the ladder. She threw herself onto Boone, gripping him tightly. "Ohmigod, you had me scared, you were down for so long. I know you can hold your breath for a dog's age, but still…"

"Nathan was kind enough to share. But we ended up pretty damn deep, so had to take it slow coming back."

Emily released him, stepping back with a smirk. "Not sure if PADI would approve of your diving apparel there, Booney-boy. Nate, if Boone's boxers treated you to an unexpected peekaboo, you have my sincere apologies."

"Yeah, put on some pants, *cabrón*," Ricardo said, tossing Boone's cargo shorts to him.

I managed an exhausted laugh, but my focus drifted to my wife's laptop bag. It had been unzipped and I looked inside. No laptop, no charger; only a few sodden papers within. I unzipped an inner pocket and ran my hand along the inside. A thumb drive was tucked into a little Velcroed pouch in the corner. Salt water was tremendously corrosive, but between the zipped pocket and the pouch, this little rectangle seemed to have remained dry.

"It wasn't piracy…" Boone said, pulling on his shorts.

"How do you know?" Emily asked.

"They sank their prize," he replied. "Looked like they blew a hole in the hull with an explosive in the bilge. Also, there was plenty of stuff onboard that looked to be of value. The TV in the stateroom, for instance. They would've stripped it."

"The stateroom?" Emily cocked her head, before going rigid. "You freedived inside a sinking ship? Are you *mental*?" She slapped a stinging palm on Boone's bare chest, eliciting a surprised yelp and leaving a handprint.

A phone rang and Emily looked into the recessed top of the camera table. "This your mobile, Nate?" she asked, bringing it to me.

"Yeah, thanks." I took it, looking at the screen. The number was "Unknown." I answered it. "Hello?"

"I thought I told you to go home, Mr. Fitzgerald," came a stern, familiar voice.

"Maybe I am home, Agent Foster. Unless you're tracking me, somehow."

"Take off the tinfoil hat, Fitzgerald. We're all on the same side. Detective Whittaker told me you were coming to Cozumel. What I'd like to know is how you knew to come here. And why?"

I decided not to mention the airport announcement I'd overheard. "It was a hunch, based on the direction the sailboat was headed."

"Lucky hunch. I'm actually here, myself. How about you meet me at the dock at the Secret Aura Hotel."

"Where's that?"

"Ask the two divemasters you're with. It's part of the complex their condo's in."

"How did you—?"

"See you in fifteen minutes," Foster interrupted, then ended the call.

Agent Foster didn't look like an FBI agent... at least not the ones I knew from television and movies. He was dressed in a lightweight tropical shirt and slacks, a pair of aviators shielding his eyes beneath his salt-and-pepper hair. While Boone and Ricardo ran bow and stern lines to the cleats, Emily killed the engine, and I stepped across to the wooden pier.

"We've been monitoring Harbor Master chatter," Foster said without preamble. "Heard about the sailboat..." His unasked question hung in the air.

"She wasn't aboard."

He nodded. "We have reason to believe she was taken off before they sank it."

"I have reason to believe that, too. I saw the Cigarette boat racing away. So, either she wasn't on the sailboat to begin with, or she's on the go-fast that went north."

Foster's aviators suddenly dipped, their mirrored lenses aimed at my side. "That what I think it is?" He pointed to what I held in my hand.

"It's Grace's laptop bag. But it's empty." I handed it to him. "Just some papers inside."

Foster took some of the sodden sheets out and glanced at them, muttering "Damn," under his breath before returning them to the bag.

I looked at Agent Foster, wondering what was going on behind the aviators. I didn't know why, but suddenly I was secure in my decision to have stashed the flash drive in my pocket. "If you knew the boat was coming here, why didn't you have someone out there to intercept it?"

"We didn't know it was coming here. Not for sure."

"And yet, here you are."

Boone and Emily stepped up beside me. I nodded to them. "Boone and Emily, this is Mr. Foster."

"Special Agent Foster," he corrected. "Of the FBI."

"Oh, cool, haven't met one of those," Em said.

"*Special Agent* Foster here," I began, stressing the title I still wasn't sure was accurate, "was about to tell me why he was here in Cozumel."

"That's classified." Foster's mirrored aviators reflected my determined face as he stared at me.

"Give me something, Foster. This is my wife we're talking about!"

Foster thought for a moment, then sighed. "Fine. We believe your wife's senior status and inside knowledge of the workings of CyberWard is likely why she was targeted."

"So... she's been kidnapped?"

"Mr. Fitzgerald, we have no way of knowing if your wife is even..." He left the thought unfinished.

"No. She's alive. I know it." I turned to Boone. "Where did Ricardo say the Cigarette boat was headed?"

"Well, he thought it was going across to Playa del Carmen. But that thing was topping fifty knots. It would be there already."

"Actually, it can go faster than that," Ricardo said, approaching the group, his eyes glued to his smartphone.

My uncle knows the Harbor Master. He said it was berthed across in Playa this morning but has not returned. The log showed it as a Cigarette 59 Tirranna, capable of over sixty-two knots."

"Bloody hell, they could be in Cancún by now!" Em gasped. "Or Isla Mujeres."

"Or farther," Ricardo said. "If they drop back to cruising speed, it's got a range of nearly 800 miles."

"We've got to get after them!" I cried.

"You need to leave this to us," Foster said, his tone taking on a military edge. "Go home to Key Largo. If your wife tries to contact you, she might do so through one of your neighbors. We've got this well in hand."

"The boat my wife was on just sank to the bottom of the sea! How do you define 'in hand'?"

Foster turned away and headed toward shore. "Go home, Mr. Fitzgerald," he called back over his shoulder. "If I find you playing detective again, I'll hit you with obstruction of an active investigation."

"Bit of a wanker, that one," Emily muttered under her breath.

I stood there, at a loss. "Those other places you mentioned... can you get me there?"

Boone sighed. "We'd need to refuel... and that boat at that speed... it would be gone by the time we got there."

"Wait... in your condo, do you have a computer I can use?"

"Of course," Em said.

"Good." I took out the flash drive. "Hope the seawater didn't destroy this."

"You took it out of the bag and didn't tell Special Agent Stick-up-his-bum?" Em asked.

"I don't trust him," I said.

"Good call," Boone said. "I only just met him and I don't trust him either."

Halfway back to the condo, my phone rang. The country code indicated it was a call from the Cayman Islands, so I thumbed the Talk icon. "Nathan Fitzgerald."

"Mr. Fitzgerald, this is Detective Whittaker in Grand Cayman. Sorry to disturb you, but… may I ask, are you still in Cozumel?"

"Yes. Why are you calling? Have you found Grace?"

"I'm afraid not, Mr. Fitzgerald, but I have some new information that I felt I should share with you."

"I'm with some of AJ Bailey's friends. Okay if I put this on speaker?"

"As you wish. I should make it clear that what I've discovered may be unrelated to your situation, but I don't believe in coincidences. Cozumel being a possible destination of your wife's sailboat struck me as… odd. I knew Agent Foster was going there, but he was far from forthcoming about his reasons."

"Sounds familiar. We just met with him."

"Really? Interesting. May I ask what the gist of that interview was?"

"Butt out and leave it to the FBI."

Whittaker grunted. "That is essentially what he told me. Nevertheless, I decided I'd reach out to a contact I have with INTERPOL, asking him if anything had crossed his desk regarding Cozumel or the Yucatán. After consulting their Central America department, he informed me that a wanted criminal with a very specific skill set was in-country. Apparently, this individual was flagged coming into Cozumel International Airport the same morning the EPIRB beacon was activated."

"Who is he?"

"He goes by several aliases," Whittaker replied. "He is a high-level hacker, specializing in industrial espionage. Given your wife's line of work, I thought this might be of interest. I'd be remiss if I didn't urge you to seek help from the proper authorities, Mr. Fitzgerald… but that being said, I'll send you the information I have."

"Are you going to share this with Foster?"

The phone was silent for a moment, then: "If I can verify he's with a proper authority."

I provided Whittaker an email and thanked him before hanging up.

Back at the condo, Em set me up in a corner with a small laptop. Fortunately, it wasn't one of those newfangled pretty ones that sacrificed function for form; this one had a standard USB port.

I plugged in the flash drive and clicked on its icon when it appeared. A number of folders were within, most with innocuous names; documents folders labeled by type and photo folders labeled by event. One of these caught my eye: "Venice, 2019." We'd never been to Venice…

I opened the folder, half-expecting to see photos of Grace with the mysterious Brandon. Instead, a single executable file lay within, labeled "Nathan." I double-clicked it and a window opened with a username and password log-in. The username was already filled in, reading "Goofus." *Ohmigod, my pet name for her when she's acting silly… and she always came back at me with…* "Doofus," I typed.

The window closed.

"Crap!"

"What is it?" Em asked, coming over. "Something wrong?"

"I think I just locked myself out of something…" My smartphone dinged with a tinkling chime, a strange notification sound I'd never heard before. I frowned and took it out. "What the…?"

A notification bar was on my phone, reading: "Press here, Doofus."

I did. The smartphone screen filled with a video. Grace looked into the camera, a smile on her face.

"Nathan. If you're watching this and everything is all right… then quit snooping in my stuff! But if something has happened to me, well… this is a little insurance policy. There have been some strange things going on at CyberWard and I'm not sure who to trust. My laptop… you know, the one with all the nerdy stickers I've stuck on the lid? It's full of very sensitive information, and I've embedded a background tracking app into the operating system. If someone tries to access it without my log-in sequence, the laptop will transmit its location through any available uplink. Once this video ends, you'll see a new application I snuck onto your phone. It's a tracking program that will indicate any pings from the laptop. I've dumbed it down, so even a Doofus can use it. Nathan… I love you."

The video ended and the phone's screen blurred as my eyes filled with tears.

"Oh, Nathan…" Em hugged me from over my shoulders.

Boone pointed at my phone. "You've got something blinking there. Is that the tracker?"

"No…" I said, wiping my eyes and taking a deep breath. "Voicemail." I tapped it and listened. A near-hysterical voice assaulted my ear.

'Mr. Fitzgerald! I've been trying to reach your wife, Grace, but she doesn't answer. This is Kim Robinson, her friend in the BVI? I recommended Brandon Wiles to help crew the trip to Nassau. Ohmigod, Nathan… Brandon was found dead in his apartment! Who's on the boat with her?'

PART III

9

As I climbed aboard the jet in Cozumel destined for Miami, my feet felt more numb with every step. Happy faces from sated tourists at the end of their vacations filled every row as I stumbled down the jet's long aisle, my hips bumping into corners of seats, and my shoulders caroming into passengers stowing luggage. My eyes were focused on my destination in the last row. Another middle seat, this time between two burly men that reeked of booze and cigarettes, and would no doubt either drink their way home, or pass out and snore stereo into my ears.

I squeezed past the guy on the aisle, his sunburned nose aglow like he was ready to guide the plane tonight, and the outline of his sunglasses bronzed onto his cheeks and forehead surrounding his white eye sockets. His perspiration-soaked fishing shirt burned my nose. I collapsed into the seat and didn't even try to fight for armrest space.

The race to Grand Cayman, chasing the signal from the jettisoned EPIRB, followed by the spontaneous flight to Cozumel that led to finding the *Anegada Da Vida* as it sank into the Caribbean Sea, left me drained beyond anything I'd ever felt before.

My hopes sank with the Island Packet when Boone and I abandoned it more than a hundred feet down with nothing more than Grace's empty computer bag.

But it hadn't been completely empty, the thumb drive with the shocking content I'd later found on it, then the frantic voicemail from Kim, had sucked any remaining confidence out of me.

My last hope was centered on the prayer that Grace was alive aboard the silver go-fast boat that had sped away just before we'd arrived. If not, then they could have dumped her body anywhere from the Virgin Islands to Mexico, and I'd never get the chance to hold her again, to kiss her lips, to…

The thought caused me to shudder, and with my arms pinned to my sides, I couldn't even wipe the tears from my cheeks. My neighbor on the aisle glanced at me from the corner of his eye, shrugged and faced forward to stare up the length of the now clear aisle. My eyes followed his gaze ahead just in time to see a late passenger dash on board.

Special Agent Foster.

Still clad in his lightweight tropical shirt, slacks, and aviator sunglasses—Foster was no doubt the kind of guy who would wear sunglasses inside the plane the entire flight. He immediately plopped down in the front row, First Class seat. FBI agents must have better perks than I would have thought, especially with last minute bookings.

When the flight attendant closed the entry door, the pre-flight announcements began. I crossed my arms and debated whether to go speak with Foster during the flight.

Exhaustion washed over me, my head slumped forward

and I fell deep into a dream state, reliving moments from the past couple days, underwater, fighting currents, indigo depths, sensations of plummeting into blackness within the sailboat, only to awake with a jump as the plane touched down hard on the runway. Startled, I was unsure where I was…

Miami.

Alone.

Grace was gone.

I wiped drool from my chin, and the passenger to my left, a younger man, straightened up and rotated his shoulder—had my head been rested there? Based on the soreness in my neck, it must have been.

The plane had come to a halt at the gate before I remembered Foster was up front. Why had he come to Miami instead of staying on the hacker's trail? Foster had ordered me to return to Florida, but he'd never said where he had originated from, so why did he come to Miami?

That thought sat me up straight. I turned my cell phone on, and the app that Grace had snuck onto it had a number two illuminated on its icon. I clicked it with my thumb, and a map appeared. As a Floridian and a boater, the Florida Straits were familiar territory, so when I saw that the first flashing beacon was on northern Cuba, my eyes bugged wide. I thumbed the blinking icon and the view zoomed in on Marina Hemingway, just outside of Havana.

"What the heck?" Even though it was a whisper, both of my neighbors glanced at me. I tried to peer forward toward Foster, but the aisle was now full of people retrieving luggage, or standing by their seats, so I could only see a few rows ahead.

The beacon suddenly minimized, and another lit up just

north of Havana. I noticed my hand shaking as I clicked on that and it zoomed in to a spot thirty miles north of Cuba, in the open waters of the Straits. I spread my thumb and index finger apart on the screen to zoom the map out and saw that the beacon appeared to be headed toward Key West. My breath caught in my chest.

Key West?

My plan had been to reluctantly follow Foster's orders, pick up my car here at the airport and drive the hour south to my home in Key Largo and await news. But what do I do now? To drive to Key West would normally take a good four hours, best case, and based on the speed of the go-fast boat, and the limited time it had been in Havana, what if it stopped there and then left again? I'd never make it to Key West in time.

The guy next to me stood up, but the aisle was still packed. Inspiration hit and I popped open my American Airlines app, and quickly found that there was a flight leaving for Key West from the same terminal where we were now in just over an hour, which given that I had to get through Customs could be tight. What would I do when I got there? Whether I flew or drove up and down the Keys, my only hope was to track the damned water rocket on Grace's tracker, so might as well fly. Concerned that all of the other last-minute flights had already maxed out my credit card, I used my backup card. The interest rate was brutal, but at this point nothing else mattered. I bought a ticket.

When finished, an idea popped into my head. "Buck Reilly!"

"Excuse me?" the guy to my left said. "Mind getting up?"

The aisle was now moving. "Yeah, sorry."

I scrolled through the directory on my phone as I walked forward and wrestled with my backpack and duffel bag, as a new urgency pressed me against the back of my other neighbor's smelly fishing shirt. I found the listing. "Last Resort Charter and Salvage," I said.

Fishing shirt glimpsed back at me. "Sounds desperate," he said.

"You have no idea."

Grace and I had gone to Key West a half-dozen years ago and stayed at the La Concha Hotel where the concierge set us up for a custom charter out to Fort Jefferson aboard an antique Grumman Widgeon flying boat. The plane was in the midst of being restored, but the pilot, Buck Reilly, was a great guy. The trip had been a blast. Buck had once been a famous archeologist who had found the tomb of the Mayan Serpent King, among many other things, before his company had gone bankrupt and he'd fled to Cayo Hueso —Key West—to hit restart on his life. His successes as an archeologist had been celebrated globally, but then diminished due to his legal battles and personal woes. If he was still living in Key West, and was available, he could be the answer I needed to find the go-fast boat.

Finally off the plane, I ran ahead of the passengers in front of me and continued toward Customs. There was no sign of Foster, but feds probably had their own shortcuts. His admonition threatening to arrest me for obstruction of an active investigation did nothing to deter my next move as I ran forward. I stabbed the number open in my directory with my finger and held the phone to my ear as I fought to keep the duffel bag on my shoulder. Phones were prohibited in Customs so I hoped he answered fast.

After four rings I'd lost hope, and then a voice finally answered. "Last Resort."

"Is this Buck Reilly?" My breathless pant must have caused him to pause.

"Who's calling?"

"Nathan Fitz… gerald…" I huffed as I ran. "My wife… Grace… and I… chartered you out to… Fort Jeff… a few… years… ago."

After a long pause where I imagined the wheels turning in Buck's head, he cleared his throat. "You okay there, Nathan?"

"Yes—I mean, no!" I stopped and sucked in a deep breath. "Grace has disappeared, or was kidnapped, I'm not sure which, but the boat she's on now is headed toward Key West!"

More silence. "I'm sorry to hear that, but what, ah, can I—"

"I want to charter you to help me find the boat. I have a tracking device—"

"Yeah, well, I'm not really doing charters these days—"

As I was deplaning, I had remembered reading that Buck had made a lucrative treasure discovery recently and had once again been dubbed King Buck, a nickname previously bestowed upon him at the pinnacle of his career.

"Please! This is an emergency, life or death. I'm jumping on the American flight out of MIA and will be there in a little over an hour. Can you please help me?"

A loud exhale sounded like a low growl on the line. "I was scheduled to look at houses this afternoon, but, yeah, I'm at the airport now. We can meet when you land—"

"Thank you so much!"

Once inside Customs I was aghast at the line of people

that snaked through rows of stanchions and filled the cavernous room. My heart raced as I dug my wallet out, exhaling a deep breath as I found my Global Entry card. I scanned that and my passport at a kiosk and quickly received a receipt with an indiscernible photo of myself and ran toward the escalators up to the Skytrain. Once aboard, I caught myself holding my breath as the train lumbered toward the final stop near gate D48. Back on the platform, I jumped down two levels of escalators, two steps at a time and hit the ground running again as the flight was now boarding.

10

It took ten minutes to run the dozen gates, and while my main focus was to breathe and not pass out from exertion, I'd kept my eye peeled for Special Agent Foster, half expecting to find him on the flight to Key West. Once down the steps to the row of gates, I saw there were no more passengers waiting to exit the terminal and walk toward the walkway to boarding area C. A ticket agent was face down into her computer by the door, no doubt closing out the flight. A flight attendant stood next to her awaiting the paperwork that noted the final headcount for the flight.

"Wait! I'm on the flight to Key West."

The agent scowled, then scanned the pass on my phone and pointed me out the glass door and to the left toward boarding area C. The planes here were accessed via fixed or rollaway stairs, which I breathlessly climbed, then stumbled onto the plane. Everyone was seated, and fortunately, this time my seat was just behind First Class on the aisle. I dropped into it like a lead weight. There was no sign of Foster. Was that good, or bad news?

The flight was brief, and what normally would be a pleasant exercise in naming the islands of the Keys as we passed over them, was a nail biter instead as I tried to recollect details about Grace's job, recent projects—she never spoke in detail—but occasionally shared perceptions of coworkers, which were rarely positive. Nothing specific jumped out at me, but I did recall a sense of discomfort that had persisted not long before she'd left for the Virgin Islands to pick up our new boat. She hadn't been sleeping well, and in fact had resorted to taking sleep aids to make it through the night. Having long ago accepted that she couldn't discuss her work, I'd given up asking questions, which I now regretted.

She, on the other hand, loved inquiring about the teams I'd been coaching at the high school, which I would explain in great detail to offset her need for confidentiality.

We landed without issue at Key West International Airport, and several vacationers aboard broke into applause and cheering. I jumped up as soon as the seatbelt light was turned off and hurried ahead of the three rows of First Class passengers, earning grimaces and shakes of their heads. When the door opened, I was the first out onto the stairway.

Down below, I spotted a tall muscular man at the bottom of the gangway talking to a deputy sheriff. Shorts, flip-flops, tanned legs, blue Last Resort T-shirt, deep-water tanned arms and face, and shoulder-length, shaggy, sun-streaked hair. His eyes were hidden by aviator sunglasses.

Buck Reilly.

I hadn't seen him in several years, but I'd remembered Grace ogling his good looks, despite his ever-professional demeanor and doing his best to ignore her doe-eyed stares.

Our eyes connected as I turned the corner on the walkway toward him. "Nathan?"

I nodded, my voice suddenly choked up. We shook hands and Buck turned to the deputy. "Thanks, Bobby, we'll cut across the tarmac to the private aviation hangar if it's okay with you."

The deputy, a tall man wearing a hat, long sleeves, and pants protecting him from the sun, nodded. "No problem, Buck. See you around."

I followed Buck past a commuter plane operated by Silver Airways, and through a gate to where private jets, seaplanes for island tours, and double- and single-engine aircraft were tied down. Over by a hangar, I spotted his Grumman Widgeon that Grace and I had chartered years ago. It looked much better now than it had then, even though there was someone on top of the wing with a hatch to one of the engines open. Uh oh.

Behind the Widgeon was a larger Grumman of similar vintage. There were a few lawn chairs sitting between them, along with an ice chest. Buck pointed to one of the chairs. "Grab a seat." He paused. "Beer? Water?"

I accepted the latter, guzzled half of it, and then he sat next to me in one of the red lawn chairs. "Congrats on your most recent discovery," I said. "One of the missing ships of the 1715 fleet, wasn't it? I saw you on the news being interviewed."

"Oh, yeah, thanks. That was, ah, pretty special."

"And you've been re-crowned as King Buck—"

"No, no, no." He waved his hand from side to side. "That's just BS the press likes to use to make people watch their shows. Kind of like the paranoia promotion that accompanies hurricanes, or the mere thought of a hurricane."

"Very true," I said. "I don't know if you remember, but Grace and I live in Key Largo, so we're used to the network hype designed to fixate everyone on their televisions whenever a system rolls off the coast of Africa."

The mechanic who had been working on the Widgeon's engine appeared on the tarmac, walked over, dug a frosty Coors Light from the ice chest and sat next to us.

"This is Ray Floyd, my partner at Last Resort."

I smiled at him and then felt my heart skip a beat as I prepared to explain what had happened.

"So, you said on the phone that Grace is missing, or maybe even kidnapped?" Buck said.

I glanced at Ray. He was wearing a red Hawaiian-print shirt and reminded me of the actor, Zach Galifianakis. Same round build, mop of dark hair and bushy beard, plus his expression was deadly serious.

"Sounds crazy, I know, but yes, that's right."

Ray's eyes grew wide and he swiveled his head to glance at Buck with a silent expression that spoke volumes of trepidation. Buck ignored him.

"Has there been a call for ransom? Are the authorities involved?"

I shook my head. "No, nothing like that. We invested most of our savings in our sailboat—" Overcome by the vision of it sinking off the coast of Cozumel, my chest heaved, and I sucked in a breath, held it and tried to stem off the tears now brimming in my eyes.

Ray leaned in and watched me so closely I thought he might fall off his chair. They refrained from asking any more questions until I regained my composure thanks to some deep breathing.

"It's okay, take your time," Buck said.

Once I could breathe normally, I walked them through the torrent of details of the past few days. Buck and Ray asked no questions, but watched my face intently the entire time, nodding occasionally, grimacing others, and shaking their heads at the end when I shared that Foster had threatened to arrest me if I got in his way.

"Foster, you say?" Buck said.

"Yeah, total jerk."

"No surprise there." Buck concurred. "I'm well acquainted with the special agent in charge of Florida and the Caribbean, so I can check with him if that's helpful." Buck's lip curled. "He's quite a piece of work himself."

Still on the edge of his seat, Ray had not broken his stare from my face. "Why would someone kidnap your wife and not ask for a ransom?"

"Because they must be after something greater than our scant savings." My statement hung in the air and did nothing to placate Ray's intense stare.

Buck leaned forward. "Like what?"

"Grace is a senior coder for a company called CyberWard."

Ray's eyes opened wider, his brow furrowed, and he sat back in his chair. Buck's eyes shifted from mine to Ray's, hesitated there, and then back to me. "What's CyberWard?"

"It's a government contractor," Ray said. "Haven't heard anything about them for a while, but they were connected to private military companies, like Blackwater, during the Gulf War." His face grew even more serious as he spoke. I squirmed in my chair; afraid his epiphany would scare Buck off.

"Like I said, she's just a coder—"

"A senior coder, you said—"

"Easy, Ray," Buck said. He cleared his throat. "Is that the kind of work she's involved with, private military companies?"

I shook my head emphatically. "No, not at all. CyberWard changed their business model after the Gulf War and diversified into a lot of different areas—mind you, Grace never told me what she was working on, but there's no way it would have been anything like that."

Ray again turned to Buck and I could see the corner of his mouth bend into a frown. A private jet taxied past us, behind the Widgeon and the seaplanes, where it came to a stop.

"Listen, I don't know what her latest projects were, but she was not emotionally invested in her work. She's very talented at coding, smarter than hell—certainly the brains of our relationship—I'm a football coach at Coral Shores High School in Tavernier, but she's the most ethical person I know. And she once told me that she didn't even know the end-use of her work as CyberWard compartmentalized their projects to prevent corporate espionage."

"Or state-sponsored espionage," Ray said.

I winced at his statement and wished I'd taken a beer rather than the water.

"That's enough, Ray," Buck said. "This isn't one of your shoot-em-up video games."

The engines were still idling on the private jet that had come to a stop at the end of the tarmac, but I noticed the passenger door and stairway slowly drop open. Ray was whispering something in an urgent tone to Buck, and I was about to plead Grace's case further, but the words stuck in my throat when I saw who deplaned from the jet.

"Oh shit," I said.

Ray spun back around to face me. "What's wrong?"

The door on the jet lifted closed, and Special Agent Foster, still wearing his shades and tropical clothing, hurried toward the private aviation terminal fifty yards to our right. I lifted my hand up to cover my face.

"Nathan?" Buck said.

"It's him. Agent Foster." My voice was a whisper.

Their chairs screeched as they turned to see Foster walking toward the private terminal. The engines on the jet began to increase in power and it started to turn around and taxi back up toward the end of the runway. "The guy off the jet?" Buck said.

"Yes. He was on my flight from Cozumel to Miami—in First Class, but I was in steerage and he didn't see me. I wondered if he'd be on my flight down here, but I never saw him." As Foster came clearly into sight, I lifted my phone and took a few rapid photographs so I could zoom in and show him to Buck and Ray.

"You say he's FBI?" Buck said.

"That's what he said."

Buck grunted loudly. "No way he works under my contact, Booth, who runs the show in these parts."

I checked the photos—there were six of Foster, but only two were clear, and in one, two thirds of his face was visible as he'd glanced partially in our direction.

"Tell me again what brought you here to Key West, and why Agent Foster would be here too?"

I bit my lip but opened the tracking app and immediately spotted a three on the icon indicating new GPS marks.

"Grace has tracking software on her computer that transmits its location onto my phone if someone is trying to access her data without the proper credentials."

The marks were in a straight line from Cuba to Key West. I clicked the closest one and saw that it was now on the northern coast of the island.

"Can I see that?" Ray said. He took the phone and studied the app. There were no commercial aspects to it, no fancy logos, no directory of options, no instructions, just a map with a trail of breadcrumbs from Havana north.

"Some kind of spyware," he said.

"Would Foster have that?" Buck said.

"No way. Grace installed it secretly. CyberWard doesn't even know."

"Unless they'd bugged your phone," Ray said.

My mouth fell open.

Buck jumped up. "Come on, Nathan. My truck is outside. Let's see if we can follow your friend, Agent Foster."

"Are you crazy, Buck?" Ray said. "These guys are heavy players!"

The smile that came across Buck's face was the most heartwarming thing I'd seen in days. "And they'll never see us coming," he said.

11

"What the hell do you want, Reilly?" The voice on Buck's speakerphone sounded anything but friendly.

"Special Agent Booth, do you always have to be so rude when I call you?" Buck said. He pumped his eyebrows at me as if he enjoyed tormenting the federal officer. We had spotted Foster climb into the backseat of a black Escalade and were following at a safe distance as it drove west along the beach away from the airport.

"That's because our arrangement is for me to call you to do things for me, not the other way around. I've told you not to use this number for anything but—"

"Emergencies, that's right, Booth. And that's exactly why I'm calling you."

"What kind of emergency do you have on that godforsaken rock you call home? The ice machine's broken? The daiquiri machine is jammed?"

I watched as Buck shifted gears on the ancient Land Rover—a Series 2A, he'd said when we'd climbed in. Built in 1966, it was older than me, and looked like it had been through hell and back.

"Do you have an Agent Foster on your all-star roster, Booth?"

"What the hell kind of question is that—do you think we give out the names of our—"

"And would he have been jetting around from Cozumel, Mexico to Miami in First Class, and then Miami to Key West on a private jet?"

"Are you insane, Reilly? Why would we have an agent—"

"Does the name Grace Fitzgerald mean anything to you?"

"One of your girlfriends, I presume?"

"She works for CyberWard."

Booth fell silent for a long moment, and then said, "Who is she, what about her, and what does she do for CyberWard?" His voice was all business now.

I caught Buck's eye. "She disappeared a few days ago on her sailboat while in the Virgin Islands. Her husband is with me now and we're trying to find her."

"Listen to me, Reilly. I have no idea who Grace Fitzsimmons is—"

"Fitzgerald—"

"But CyberWard is not to be messed with. If she works there and has gone missing, that's serious business."

"No shit, Booth. That's why I called you. It's an emergency."

"No, hotshot," Booth said. "If it involves CyberWard, it's a *national* emergency."

The Escalade turned right at the end of the beach and continued up to where a temporary stop sign had been erected. Road construction was ahead, and all traffic was directed to detour to the left. We followed them through the stop sign, with two cars in between us.

"What about Agent Foster?" I said.

"Who is that on the line, Reilly?"

Buck signaled me to respond. "Nathan Fitzgerald, sir. Grace's husband."

"Are you in law enforcement?" Booth said.

His question took me aback. "No, I'm a football coach in the Keys."

"Jesus Christ. A football coach and treasure hunter. Perfect."

The Escalade stopped at another intersection. There was a long concrete pier to the left. And to the right was White Street, where they turned. One car continued straight through the stop sign, the other turned right behind the Escalade, and we followed.

"We're behind Foster now," Buck said. "He was picked up in a black SUV with tinted windows and is presently headed north on the island." Buck paused. "Is he one of yours, or not?"

A loud exhale caused distortion on the phone. "No, he's not one of mine, which means he's dangerous and you men need to back off and let me scramble some help."

I shook my head from side to side and pointed toward the Escalade.

"Negative, Booth. Nathan's wife has a tracking device on her computer and it sends a location to Nathan's phone whenever anyone tries to access her data without her password."

"And?"

"And it's been pinging steadily since a silver Cigarette

boat fled the scene of her sailboat getting scuttled in Cozumel, Mexico, this morning. They've left a trail from there to Havana and are now pulling into Key West."

Booth was quiet for a moment. "Havana? Was the wife found on the sailboat?"

"No, I dove it myself. She wasn't there," I said.

Buck had to speed up to make the light at Truman—it turned yellow—he downshifted and floored the ancient Land Rover. The light turned red, but we made it through, nobody honked at us, and no police cars were in sight. The Escalade continued up White Street.

"So could she be on the Cigarette boat?" Booth said.

I leaned closer to the phone. "That's what I'm hoping for, and why I asked Buck to help—"

"Could she be involved?"

His words hit me like a sledgehammer and I ground my teeth in anger at the accusation. "I know my wife, and there's no way."

"Nathan?" Buck's voice refocused me away from Booth, who had just questioned whether my wife was a criminal. "Text me the photos you took of Foster at the airport and I'll send them to Booth." He then held the phone closer to his mouth. "Run them through your database, Booth, and then call me back—"

"Don't tell me what to do, Reilly! And you don't have the appropriate clearance for—"

"We need to go. The Escalade just turned left on Eaton Street and may be headed toward Key West Bight. Hundreds of boats there, maybe he's intercepting the Cigarette—"

"No, wait! Reilly?"

"I'll share my location with you—for today only—so

you can send help." Buck glanced to me, then back at the phone. "Pronto, please."

"Don't tell me—"

Buck hit the end button and the phone fell silent. I checked our location on Google Maps. Foster's vehicle had turned right on Grinnell Street and then left on Caroline Street, one block from and parallel to Key West Bight, the biggest marina complex in Key West. After two more blocks west, they turned right on William Street and drove past a large parking lot.

Buck slapped his palm on the top of his steering wheel. "Either they saw us and are turning down the one-way alley behind Schooner Wharf, or Foster's getting dropped off at the end of the street by the water." He slapped the steering wheel again as the Escalade pulled to a stop in the circle at the end of the road. Buck turned right up a narrow, nameless street, accelerated, and pulled into the large parking lot.

"Let's go," he said.

"What if he sees us?" I said.

"Based on the Cigarette's arrival here, it seems Foster must be connected, otherwise he wouldn't be showing up alone—assuming he was getting dropped at the end of the street in a very public location." Buck jumped out of the Land Rover.

I slammed my door and hurried after him. "So?"

"So we have no choice but to flush him out," Buck said. "If we spot Grace, we'll play it by ear."

"Do you think they have guns, Buck? Do we have guns?"

He laughed at my question, which, based on him being attired in flip-flops, shorts, and a tight shirt, was a foolish one.

"We'll keep our distance," he said. "I'm not planning on getting shot today."

I felt my heart accelerate as we hurried past some dumpsters and between two buildings that brought us to a wooden boardwalk that went east and west along the waterfront. Restaurants, T-shirt shops, and a public bathroom were on one side, and countless boats of all sizes were on the other. Finger docks extended far into the harbor, and I hesitated a moment and searched for the silver Cigarette.

Buck was looking at his phone and held it up for me to see. "I sent that picture of Foster to Booth. He said he'll run it through the Bureau's database." He enlarged the picture by touching his screen and spreading his fingers apart, and then held it up closer to his face.

"Come on," he said. "Let's go this way."

I followed Buck up the boardwalk toward where the street ended in a cul-de-sac where the Escalade had stopped. We peered around the corner of a T-shirt shop at the end and saw that the vehicle was gone. Damn.

"Nathan!"

The voice came from the waterside of the boardwalk. I looked over and saw Foster on a bright yellow go-fast boat that appeared to be thirty-five feet long and had four 350-horsepower outboards on its transom.

"What the hell are you doing here?"

There were two other men, all dressed in black, on the boat with Foster. None were smiling. He jumped off the boat and onto the dock, approaching me.

"Are you following me?" he said.

"No, I, er—"

Buck stepped forward and between the oncoming tropically clad, sunglass-wearing man who had been representing himself as an FBI agent, and me.

Out of patience, running on nothing but adrenalin, I bit my lip, ready to lunge for him and beat him senseless until he told me where my wife was, but the backward glance Buck gave me indicated that he'd handle it.

Foster's eyes were fixed on me, and he was coming in fast. Buck put his hands out toward the center of Foster's chest—Foster started to reach for them, then stopped. I got the sense that he was ready to throw down some martial arts on Buck but recognized the public setting.

"Back off," Buck said. "The man's wife has been kidnapped."

Foster sneered at Buck. "Who the hell are you? The high school math teacher?"

"This is Buck Reilly, he's a charter pilot," I said.

Foster turned back to me. "We think Grace is a part of what's happening. A co-conspirator. Now I won't tell you again. Go home or we'll assume you're involved, too."

I stepped toward him. "Involved in what, Foster?"

"It's a need-to-know situation, Nathan. Sorry. But I'm hot on their tail—"

"Buck has a seaplane and we can help search—"

"What?" Foster stepped back and a smart-ass grin tightened his face. "Oh, *that* Buck Reilly, the treasure hunter who flies around in antique airplanes." His smile turned to a sneer. "No big payday here, pal. You can back off, too."

"Mind showing me your credentials, Foster?" Buck said.

"Fuck off, Reilly."

After a long glance, he stepped back aboard the yellow go-fast boat, and the man at the helm whispered something to him and started the four engines. The collective rumble and vibration sounded like a SpaceX rocket leaving the launch pad. We watched as they cast off and idled out into the harbor. A sudden urge caused me to check Grace's tracking app on my phone but no new signals had registered. The last one was very close to here though.

Buck's phone rang and he pulled it out of his pocket. "It's Booth, maybe he's found something about Foster."

He placed the phone against his ear and listened for a moment before his eyes went wide and his mouth dropped open.

"Oh shit," Buck said.

12

People walked past us by the dozen, some laughing, a few drinking beers, others lining up to board sunset cruises, and none noticing that my world was on the brink of destruction. My eyes were locked onto Buck's, and his remained wide. He'd not uttered a word since Booth had shared whatever news he had. The phone was still pressed to his ear.

"What's he saying?" I said.

Buck's eyes fluttered, he shook his head once, and then grabbed me by the arm and walked at a brisk pace back the way we'd come.

"How certain are you of this, Booth?"

I couldn't hear the conversation, but whatever the response had been, Buck clenched his teeth and pulled me harder down the boardwalk. Finally, when we turned the corner between the buildings and were nearly back to where we'd left the Land Rover, he stopped and put the phone on speaker.

"Booth, you're on speaker now. Tell Nathan what you told me."

Booth cleared his throat. "I'm sorry to tell you this, Mr. Fitzgerald, but the man you know as Foster is really named Stanley Hyde. He is by no means a Special Agent for the Federal Bureau of Investigation, quite the opposite, actually." I glanced at Buck and then back at the phone. "Hyde is a former Delta Force sniper, gone rogue, and now a known assassin."

I sucked in a deep breath and lost my balance momentarily, spun on the ball of one foot and the heel of the other. Buck grabbed my shoulder and held me steady.

"He's been connected previously to Russian oligarchs who operate outside the law in their own country but generate so much capital overseas and grease enough palms in the motherland, they're left alone. We're not sure of the connection to CyberWard yet, but we have people on their way to the company's headquarters in Palo Alto as we speak. They're armed with a search warrant to determine what your wife was working on."

Buck again grabbed me by the arm and steered me to his Land Rover. We climbed inside, he tossed his phone in my lap, started the engine, jammed the transmission in reverse, ground the gears as he put it in first, then launched us toward the street.

"You still there, Nathan?" Booth said. "Reilly?"

I held the phone up, still on speaker.

"We're here, Booth," Buck replied. "Great that you have agents on the way to the headquarters, but we're here on the ground, and Foster, or Hyde or whatever his name is, is in a water rocket on his way out of Key West Bight."

"Close to where the last beacon from Grace's computer registered on the tracking app," I added.

The old Land Rover was deceptively faster than it appeared, and we were now on Palm Avenue Causeway bridge shooting past a marina on the right and houseboats on the left, and then over Roosevelt Boulevard. Headed back to the airport, I guessed. I glanced at him and he rolled his index finger in a circle—hurry up, was the message.

"Don't get any crazy ideas, men," Booth said.

We cut off a car as Buck ran a red light at Flagler Avenue, and they blared their horn at us.

"Reilly, what are you doing?" Booth said. "Reilly?"

Buck took the phone from my hand and spoke into it. "We're headed to the airport, Booth. Gotta go now, but I shared my location with you—"

"Do not pursue that speedboat, Reilly! Nathan? Don't be foolish, there's nothing you can do—you'll get yourselves killed!"

"I need to make a call, Booth," Buck said. "Send the cavalry down here ASAP. Bye for now."

Buck hit end, and then pressed another speed dial button.

"Ray, it's me. Get the Beast ready to fly and start the engines for us, we'll be there in seven minutes. Don't ask questions, please, just do it!"

The Land Rover hurtled down the street that was closed for repairs, and Buck slammed on the brakes just before we went nose first into a partially filled ditch that crossed the road. He continued forward into the trench, albeit at a slower pace, until we'd climbed back out, and then accelerated again. We blew past the beach and into the one-way exit of the airport—going the wrong way, I assumed because it was closer to the private aviation terminal. I hung on for dear life, but kept my lips pressed tight rather than whine or complain because he was doing this for me.

For Grace.

He didn't bother to park the Land Rover in a spot, and we left it running in front of the small building that housed Flight Services. We ran through it like Butch Cassidy and the Sundance Kid, and out onto the tarmac where we found the propellers churning on the larger of the two Grumman planes. Ray climbed out as we approached.

"What—where are you going?"

"No time for questions, Ray." Buck came to a sudden stop. "Listen, there are two go-fast boats. The silver one fled the scene where Grace's boat sank this morning in Cozumel—and it's now here, and Foster, a.k.a. Stanley Hyde, international assassin, is on a banana yellow go-fast headed out of the Bight now. My guess is they're heading north."

Ray's jaw hung open as he glanced slowly from Buck to me.

"We're going to find my wife!"

Buck nodded emphatically once, jumped on the ladder, and climbed aboard. He stuck his head out once on board. "Mind parking my truck? It's still running out front."

I followed after him and contorted myself into the right seat in the cockpit.

"Buckle up," he told me.

Fortunately, there was no traffic and we were airborne within a minute. My eyes searched the cockpit for any modern technology, but found nothing other than World War II era gauges, knobs, handles, and accoutrements. Buck flew the plane like a champ, clearly knowing it like the back of his hand.

Once out over the water, we banked hard to port and cut back over the bridge that connected Stock Island to Key West. The sun reflected on the water, which alternated from brilliant swaths of light emerald-green to random dark patches due to the turtle grass that flourished below the surface. Low-lying islands of mangroves and thin spits of sand randomly dotted the horizon, all of which would have captivated me if the circumstances had been different.

Buck offered me a headset. I'd never flown in the cockpit of a plane. If I had more time to think about it, I may have been terrified, but the adrenalin was flowing like a fire hose, and if Buck wasn't worried, then neither was I.

"Foster's boat was on the northwest, or Florida Bay side of the Keys, but if they're headed toward Miami, they'll have to cross over to the ocean side at some point. We'll search Florida Bay up until Summerland where there's a channel they might take to the ocean. The boat, or boats, shouldn't be hard to spot as they'll both leave a wide white swath as they haul ass north." He looked over at me and we stared each other in the eye. "You keep watch out the starboard window, and I'll watch out the port. Got it?"

I nodded, and suddenly felt choked up. "Thanks, Buck."

"Don't thank me yet."

My chest was tight with appreciation, not only for Buck, but the amazing people who had helped me in Grand Cayman and then Cozumel. Professional, caring folks who had seriously gone out of their way to help their fellow man, and it had nothing to do with getting paid. I glanced for a second back to Buck—King Buck—as he had been nicknamed years ago. What I knew of his story would never lead me to believe he'd help what in essence was a total stranger. A deep breath refocused me on the search. As appreciative as I was, a nagging question continued to gnaw at me.

What will we do if we find them?

We flew for twenty minutes without seeing anything but lines of jet skis, skiffs being poled along the flats, trolling boats following a weedline, and shrimp boats on the leeward side of the islands. Soon after Buck had adjusted our course to the eastern side of the island chain, I saw his body language change.

"There you are, you sons of bitches," he said.

"What have you got, Buck?"

"Two go-fast boats, just southeast of Big Pine."

We flew over them without changing our altitude, which was 1,500 feet above sea level. I checked my phone and there was a mark located just south of here. I held it up to show him. Buck then handed me his phone and asked me to text Booth our location, and note that the boats were either traveling together, or one was chasing the other and heading northeast.

He then banked the plane on its port wingtip and crossed back over the mass of Big Pine, which was larger than most of the islands we'd flown past, continued around until we were headed south, and then cut back east again as he reduced altitude to five hundred feet. The go-fast boat in back was bright yellow, and the one ahead of it was silver.

I clenched my fists. "What's the plan?"

"We need to see if Grace is on one of those boats, and if so, we'll figure out a way to intercept them."

I glanced back out the window. The boats were close, but not close enough to make out any fine details or identify faces. "How are we going to do that?"

An evil smile preceded Buck pushing the wheel

forward. It felt as if we were on a roller coaster that had just rounded the crest and were now pointed toward the ground—or in this case, the water. I suddenly felt empathy for Buck's partner, Ray Floyd. He was clearly the cautious, rule-following type. Buck must really keep him on pins and needles.

A quarter mile back from them, Buck leveled off, and the altimeter read two hundred feet. The spray off the yellow boat's quad engines was causing a mist on the plane's windscreen. Foster/Hyde came into view. He suddenly stood, turned backwards, and pointed at us as we approached; the man who wasn't driving sprung up from his seat.

"Hey, Buck?" I said.

"You see her?"

"Not yet."

Suddenly we were over the yellow boat and blew past it with a bead on the stern of the silver one. My concern about what the man on the yellow boat was doing was forgotten in my haste to study the silver one.

Long blond hair wafted wildly in the breeze from a backseat of the boat ahead. Could it be? Is it Grace?

Buck vectored slightly to their left side and I could clearly see on board—yes!

"She's there! Grace is on the silver boat!"

My heart leapt at the sight of her as she lifted her head to gaze up at the madman pilot swooping over their heads.

"What else did you see?" Buck said.

"Two other men, one driving, and one in a passenger seat. Grace is sitting in the backseat."

"Was she tied up? Do they have guns?"

"I…I'm not sure."

With a kick of the port foot pedal and a turn of the wheel, we again cut to the left, but this time, rather than circling behind them, Buck vectored in a figure eight and approached them head-on.

"Look for details!" he said.

We swooped down low, straight toward the silver boat and I took a few quick pictures with my phone as the men hunkered down—I saw a gun protrude over the windshield—

"Gun!"

Just before Buck swerved hard to port to cut between the boats, I clearly saw Grace, her teeth gritted as she stared up at us—wait, what?

What was in her hands?

The sound of bullets ripping through the fuselage burst through my headset. Buck took sudden and repeated evasive measures—zigging and zagging every few seconds until we had circled behind the yellow boat and back toward land. More muzzle flashes erupted from that boat, and a stream of fire from multiple sources was visible from the silver boat too.

Another ear-shattering sound ripped through the fuselage behind us—a loud siren sounded from the instrument panel—an alarm of some kind!

"Crap!" Buck shouted. "Check the back."

Whether it was shock or a streak of fearlessness I didn't know I possessed, I released my lap belt, jumped out of the seat and into the back of the plane. My eyes bugged wide and I froze—several holes perforated both sides of the plane, but through the starboard side window I spotted a plume of smoke billowing behind the engine.

"Fire!"

The plane lurched to the north as Buck struggled with the wheel. He dug in his door pocket and then tossed me a small fire extinguisher, which I caught in the air.

"Not inside," I shouted. "It's the engine!"

His eyes bulged wider. The sound of the alarm continued. "We're going down!" Buck said.

I shimmied forward, fell back into the right seat, righted myself, connected my lap belt, pulled the shoulder straps over my head, and struggled to plug them into the center hub of the lap belt, but my hands were shaking so badly I couldn't push the tongue into the housing.

With my headset back on, I peered out the side window. "The smoke is getting thicker!"

"Dammit."

Buck added throttle by pressing forward the twin handles that hung down from the ceiling and pulled gingerly back on the wheel.

He then keyed the mic. "Mayday, mayday, mayday. Miami Center, Miami Center. Grumman N6236 coming into Marathon hot, I repeat, mayday, mayday, mayday, Grumman N6236 coming in hot."

"Miami Center here, Grumman. Marathon's been notified and emergency support will be waiting on the runway. Altitude alert, Grumman. You're at three hundred feet, can you make it? Over."

"Not sure, Miami Center, we're trying. Over."

I pressed my hands together and wanted to pray but couldn't take my eyes off the airport lights in the distance. I knew the four lights to the left of the runway were a glide slope indicator, and with all of them being red right now, it was a bad sign.

"Engine troubles, Grumman? Over."

"Negative, Miami Center. Starboard engine is on fire. We were fired on by two go-fast boats south of the Seven Mile Bridge, east bound, over."

"Roger that, Grumman. The Coast Guard will be notified. Over."

Buck rubbed his face and sat forward in the seat, glancing back and forth from the few gauges on the instrument panel to the airport ahead. He appeared calm but sweat dripped steadily down the side of his face.

Another fast glance out the window showed a thick stream of smoke. "You got it, Buck. Come on, man," I said.

I wrapped my arms through the safety belt and glanced around for anything I could grab hold of. After all this I didn't want to die in an antique airplane. What I saw, or thought I saw, on the silver boat as we swung back around had me numb and dizzy, which combined with the altimeter spinning counterclockwise, it was all I could do to not lose the meager contents of my stomach all over the cockpit.

"Come on, baby!" Buck shouted. "You're a beauty, just like Ray says—I only call you the Beast as an endearment!"

The runway filled the windscreen ahead of us as we dropped toward it. At the last second Buck lowered the landing gear. A fire engine burst out of a hangar, its lights flashing—I checked the cabin, and saw no smoke inside.

"You can do this, Buck!"

The ground came fast—

BOOM!

We hit hard, but stuck firm on the runway and Buck pulled back on the throttles, moved some other levers, pulled a couple knobs, and we slowed to a crawl. We both sat back hard in our seats, and I tried to slow my gasping breaths.

Good Lord.

"You okay?" he said.

"Fine, yeah, I'm fine. You?"

"I'm okay, yeah. Let's get the hell out of here!"

The smell of smoke hit fast and we both pulled off our lap and shoulder harnesses.

Buck followed my scramble into the cabin and I heard him say, "Ray's gonna kill me. Damn, damn, damn."

The fire truck caught up to us, and a sudden spray of white foam enveloped the fuselage and cockpit. It felt like we were in a car wash.

"I'm sorry I got you into this, Buck."

As he lifted the latch on the hatch, he turned to face me. "You saw Grace on the boat?"

"Yeah, I saw her. She was there." I couldn't bring myself to smile.

Buck's brow furrowed as he studied my expression. "Was she okay?"

"Yeah, she looked fine, but ah, well, I think she was holding a gun."

Buck flinched at the revelation, his eyes wide, and then, inexplicably, he began to laugh. His body shook with nervous laughter and I wondered whether he was having a breakdown, or maybe it was the reaction of a pilot who had just crash-landed after his plane was shot out of the sky. He pushed the hatch open after a moment and exhaled a hard breath.

"Okay, Nathan. I'm going to check the damage to my plane before I get grilled by the NTSB, Special Agent Booth and my business partner, so unfortunately, this is the end of the line for us."

I nodded my head. The dizziness had not subsided, and I thought it might never, given what I'd seen and been through. Now out on the tarmac we saw firemen on the other side of the plane still spraying the starboard engine and wing.

"We're in Marathon, right?" I asked.

"Yeah, that's right." Buck paused and glanced back at me. "What are you going to do?"

I shook my head. I'd come this far. "I need to learn the truth, no matter what it is."

Miraculously, Buck smiled. "It'll set you free."

"We'll see."

Then Buck's eyes narrowed and his face shifted to a thoughtful expression. "There's a guy I know that has an island near here who might be just the ticket to help you do that."

"He's got his own island?"

"Oh, he's got a lot more than that." Buck pulled his phone out of his pocket, scrolled through the contacts, and gave me a serious glance. "Whether he's here or not will be the problem. I'll call him for you."

Buck held the phone to his ear. "Jesse, it's Buck. You wouldn't happen to be in Marathon, would you?"

PART IV

13

Once the firefighters extricated us from the foam cocoon that was Buck's airplane, he pointed me toward the parking lot beyond the small terminal building.

"That's the guy," he said. "The big ugly truck pulling up by the gate. I'll take care of this mess. You go find the truth."

Looking where Buck pointed, I saw a tall man climb out of a vehicle that made Buck's Land Rover look like a fancy luxury SUV. I had no idea what it was, except old.

I turned and shook his hand. "Thanks, Buck."

Walking slowly toward the building, the adrenaline that'd been coursing through me started to dissipate and I was suddenly very tired.

In just a few days, I'd flown from Miami to Grand Cayman, to Cozumel via Miami, back to Miami, then on to Key West, and finally, to Marathon. Where we crash landed. I'd made three dives, been threatened with jail time, and been shot at by my own wife, who I was trying to rescue.

Was that what the truth was going to boil down to? That

she'd grown tired of our life in the islands and wanted more?

I was beyond exhausted.

Just outside the private aviation building sat another airplane that looked a lot like Buck's, only it was bigger and though I knew it was probably older than me, it looked brand new. On the nose was an old-fashioned drawing of a pretty, scantily dressed, young woman, gold hair flying in the wind. The name of the flying boat was *Ocean Hopper*.

As I approached the building, the tall man beside it waved me toward him. There was a gate there, which he pushed open as I approached.

"Are you Jesse McDermitt?" I asked.

He nodded and stuck out his hand, which I shook. "Yeah, Buck said your wife's in some trouble."

"Her name's Grace and she was kidnapped. I'm Nathan Fitzgerald."

He was an older guy, a little older than me, though I couldn't even begin to guess how old. He wore his hair unstylishly short, like a soldier, and there were a few grays mixed in with the sun-bleached, sandy brown. Broad shouldered and athletically built, he moved with confidence and certainty. There was something about his attitude that just screamed military.

He had a skull tattooed on his forearm, faded by the years. The skull had one of those old-style scuba regulators in its mouth with two flexible hoses, and what looked like wings for ears and crossed oars behind it.

We got into his car, or truck, or whatever it was and he started the engine, but didn't drive. The air conditioner started cooling the hot air trapped inside almost immediately.

On the outside, the old SUV looked like it belonged in a junkyard, or out in some farmer's field. There were rust streaks down the sides and though the original color had been light blue, the hood was mostly rusty brown. But the inside looked brand new, and the chug of a big diesel engine under the hood and the huge off-road tires left no doubt that it was a wolf in sheep's clothes.

A lot of locals bought cheap, throwaway cars in the Keys. The salt air made buying a new car a big risk. Mostly, they were rust buckets from the mainland and the locals called them Keys cars.

"Buck gave me a few details," he said. "He told me y'all saw her just a little while ago out on the water. With the kidnappers?"

So, I went on to explain what had happened to Grace, her last contact off Haiti, finding the EPIRB on the edge of the wall in the Caymans, watching our boat sink in Cozumel, finding the thumb drive and its contents, and the flight here with Buck.

I told him about the fake FBI agent and how Grace's boss seemed to know everything that was going on, including my whereabouts.

I intentionally left out the part about Grace holding a gun. I don't know what made me do that, maybe some hope that I'd been mistaken.

"I don't know what to do next," I said. "Their boats are just too fast to catch without an airplane and I got Buck's shot out of the sky. The FBI's working on it, but every minute takes Grace a mile farther away."

"I have planes," he said. "You just walked past one of them."

"That Grumman?"

"Grumman G-73 Mallard to be precise. Traded Buck for it, and his partner and mechanic did a full restoration."

"Ray Floyd?"

He looked over at me and nodded. "You met him?"

"Earlier today."

"What kind of boat are the kidnappers in?"

"I'm not sure," I replied, pulling my phone out.

I'd taken a few pictures of the two boats but didn't know if any were clear enough to see the manufacturer's name. I held my phone up with the best shot of the silver boat.

"Cigarette Tirranna," he said. "Saw one at the Miami Boat Show last year when they introduced it. Top speed of about sixty knots."

"Fastest boat I've ever seen."

"Fast," he agreed with a nod. "But not everything revolves around speed and that boat's a long way from being the fastest. Those boats are used by a lot of smug drugglers, just because they can outrun most anything law enforcement has on the water."

Smug Druggler? I thought. What an odd phrase.

"Why are you willing to help me?" I asked.

He turned in his seat and fixed me with a gaze that would melt cobalt. His face was tanned and lined with years, but the spark in his gray-blue eyes sent shivers down my spine.

"A turd fondler with a similar boat had my second wife abducted sixteen years ago," Jesse said. "She was murdered on our wedding night."

He put the truck in gear and slowly drove out of the airport, turning south on US 1, the famed Overseas Highway.

"How were you able to follow the boats from Coz to here?" he asked.

I pulled up the tracker app on my phone, noting two more pings. I explained what was on the thumb drive Boone and I retrieved from *Anegada Da Vida*, and how it'd activated the app Grace had secretly installed on my phone.

"She works for a tech company," I said, then showed him the tracker.

His brow furrowed. "They stopped in Havana?"

"Marina Hemingway," I replied. "Buck figured they refueled there. But the boat's supposed to have an eight-hundred-mile range."

"If they run slow, yeah. But going as fast as that picture shows, the range is probably less than a fourth of that. If they gassed up there, they might be able to make it to Miami, but doubtful if they went to Key Weird first. You said there were two boats?"

I scrolled through my images, found one of the yellow boat, and showed it to him. "This one only has four engines."

"Looks like a Fountain," he said after a quick glance. "Probably just as fast as that Tirranna, since it's not as big. Those locations on the tracker? Does it send the information every hour or some other predetermined time?"

"In the video Grace sent, she said that each time someone tries to access her laptop, it'd send a location beacon to my phone."

"She must have been nervous about her employer."

The realization hit me like a ton of bricks. I'd seen the gun in Grace's hand. I hadn't really believed it, but I'd had doubts about my wife. I'd thought she was involved. Yet, someone was still unsuccessfully trying to access her computer from the very boat she was on.

"She said as much in the video," I replied, suddenly excited, and mentally kicking myself for having doubted her. "We're not going to take your airplane?"

He looked over at me and grinned, as he made a U-turn, then turned into a driveway beside a leaning mailbox. We were instantly swallowed up by a tropical jungle.

"Planes are fast," he said. "But it's hard to stop a boat with one."

"You have a fast boat?" I asked.

He ignored my question and asked one of his own. "What else can you tell me about this place your wife works? What'd you call it? CyberWard?"

"A tech firm out of Palo Alto, California," I replied, marveling at the dense foliage the long, winding driveway passed through. "They work for the government and a number of arms manufacturers, from what she told me, providing cyber security. The FBI is raiding their offices pretty much as we speak."

"Who's the agent in charge?"

"A man named Booth," I replied. "He and Buck seemed to have a long history. From what I gathered, he's in charge of the FBI's office in Miami. He found out that the guy who'd identified himself as an FBI agent and kept pushing me to just go home, is actually a known assassin and former soldier named Stanley Hyde."

I was watching Jesse's face to gauge his response to that. He didn't look over or show any effect at all. Most people would have some sort of reaction to the word assassin.

As we pulled into a clearing, I saw that we were actually at a business of some kind, with a large grassy area beyond it, right down to the water, where another airplane was parked by a boat ramp.

There was a metal-roofed building, with a wraparound deck, full of tables and chairs, another building beyond it looked like a house, and there was a small shack down by the water's edge. There were at least fifteen boats tied up along a long canal.

He parked but didn't shut off the engine. Instead, he pulled a cell phone out and made a call.

"Hey, Chyrel, it's me," he said. "You busy?"

The main building was obviously a restaurant, but there was no sign saying the name and I hadn't seen one on the highway.

"Good," Jesse said into the phone. "I need you to find out a few things for me. First, I need to talk to an FBI special agent in charge by the name of Booth. He works out of the Miami field office. Then check on satellite availability over South Florida. I also want everything there is to know about a company in Palo Alto called CyberWard and a former spec-ops guy called Stanley Hyde."

He listened for a moment, then one eyebrow raised slightly, and he glanced over at me. "You know about them, huh? Can you hack into their system and find out all the things they don't want anyone to know?"

I heard laughter over the tiny speaker at Jesse's ear.

"Good," he said. "Get on it. Since this CyberWard might be what you think, let Jack know what's going on. We may need *Ambrosia*. And have this Booth guy contact me right away."

"Who was that?" I asked when he ended the call. "And what is this place?"

"This is the Rusty Anchor Bar and Grill," he replied.

"Owned by my friend Rusty Thurman. The person I was talking to on the phone is one of the world's top computer analysts and hackers, though she doesn't like to be called that."

"Grace is a senior coder at CyberWard," I said. "I don't know much about her work, but I remember her telling me that not even the CIA could hack their system."

"She's probably right," Jesse said, shutting off the engine. He opened the door and got out. "But Chyrel doesn't work for the CIA anymore."

I got out and followed him toward the restaurant in the gathering darkness. When we entered, I had to pause for a moment to allow my eyes to adjust to the gloomy interior. Although there were windows all the way around, and the sun was behind the trees to the west, it was still darker inside than out. The windows had real hurricane shutters, which allowed you to see out, but blocked the sunlight during the day.

Two big dogs—a yellow lab and a rottweiler—rose from a corner and came directly to Jesse. They both eyed me cautiously, as he bent slightly to scratch their ears. I noted that a man of average height probably wouldn't need to bend over at all. They were both bigger than Bogey.

"*Hola, hermano,*" a long-haired man said, sitting at the bar with several others. He didn't look Hispanic. "Where'd you run off to in such a hurry?"

"Go fire up the *Revenge*, Jimmy," Jesse said to the man. "Is she gassed up?"

"Topped the tanks when we got back," Jimmy replied, rising from his bar stool. "Put the extra fuel bladders in the fish boxes and filled them, too. Just like you told me. Where we going?"

"Chasing a Tirranna," Jesse replied.

The man stopped as he was turning away, and a slow smile came to his face. "That new Cigarette center console with six engines?"

"This one has the four hundreds," Jesse replied. "Twenty-four hundred horses. This man's name is Nathan. He's from up island—Key Largo—and his wife Grace has been taken and she's on that boat."

There were nearly a dozen people there, scattered at tables around the bar area, mostly rough-looking local men. It got quiet and several chairs scraped as a few got to their feet as one.

"Anything we can do?" one man asked.

"Thanks, Dink," Jesse said to him. "I've got it."

The man awkwardly sat back down. The others did likewise, but it remained quiet.

A short, bearded man moved from behind the bar. "Need me to go with ya, bro?" he asked, his voice sounding as Conchy as the restaurant looked.

"Oh, no you don't," a tall, full-figured redhead said. "You have work to do here."

A blond woman sitting at the bar, rose and approached Jesse. Her hair was full and wavy, streaked by sun and sea. She was tan and strikingly beautiful.

"What's going on?" she asked Jesse.

Her voice was like molasses and with just those three words, I could tell she was not just from the Deep South but old money, too.

"Nathan," Jesse said, "this is my wife, Savannah. That's Rusty behind the bar and his wife Sid, and Jimmy over by the door. The rest of this motley crew here at the Anchor are fishing guides and similar miscreants, trawler trash, and boat bums. But we look after one another. You're an islander, so that includes you and Grace."

Then he turned toward his wife and took both her shoulders in his hands. "Savvy, Nathan's wife Grace was kidnapped several days ago. They were spotted in a go-fast boat, running outside the reef just a little while ago. I'm going to help him get her back."

"I'll get the boat started," Jimmy said, then hurried out the door.

My phone rang and I looked at the screen. "It's a Miami number."

"Answer it," Jesse said.

I pushed the *Accept* button and said, "Nathan Fitzgerald."

"Who the hell is Jesse McDermitt?" Booth yelled.

14

My mind was in a haze. The constant twists and turns of the last few days, lack of sleep, my body pumping adrenaline through my veins almost constantly, the danger…

Then the emotional ups and downs; the fear of losing Grace forever, then thinking that it had all been a lie, the doubt, so many people trying so hard to help me get Grace back. And so many others, trying to stop me.

I held the phone out to Jesse. "It's Booth."

Jesse took it and held it to his ear. "McDermitt."

He listened for a moment. I could hear Booth's angry voice but couldn't make out what he was saying. The lines at the corners of Jesse's eyes grew deeper as his brow furrowed.

"Listen up, Booth," Jesse interrupted the man. "I'm only gonna say this once. Uncle Sam no longer signs my paychecks. But when he did, my chain of command was exceedingly short—a deputy director of Homeland Security, the Homeland Secretary, and the President of the United States. My current chain of command is even shorter—a man named Jack Armstrong and the SecDef—that stands for Secretary of Defense, in case you didn't know. You people up in Quantico can't even wipe your own ass without tripping over one another to check the polls to see if the general consensus is to wipe up or down. You are *not* in my chain, Booth, and if you get in my way, you'll likely end up in the Djibouti field office, pushing papers. Do I make myself perfectly clear?"

I couldn't hear anything on the other end.

"You there, Booth?" McDermitt demanded, his voice quite loud for such a public place.

Several people at surrounding tables looked over, then just went about their conversations.

Jesse listened for a moment, then said, "Good, you know who I work for. Your boss's boss has Jack's contact information. By now he's up to speed on what I'm about to do. Forward any and all information you get about Cyber-Ward to him. And Booth. Don't leave *anything* out—no redactions—or I'll come up to Miami personally for a little discussion on interagency sharing."

He ended the call and handed me my phone. I looked down at it, then up at him. "Who the hell are you?"

"I'm just a simple boat captain," he replied, then turned to his wife. "Don't worry, babe. I should be home by morning. Take Rusty's boat back to the island." Then he turned to the bearded man. "If you can get away, Rusty, I could use a hand."

He kissed his wife on the forehead, then without another word, headed toward the door Jimmy had exited through.

Savannah turned toward me. "You'd best hurry along if you want to keep up with Jesse."

"Is he always like this?" I asked.

"Focused? Intense? In command? Abrupt?" she said, with a trace of humor. "Pretty much. Except when he's angry."

"You don't want to see Jesse McDermitt pissed, man," a guy sitting at a table next to us said. He looked like a local.

I started to turn, but Savannah put a hand on my arm. She stepped toward me and gave me a warm hug. "Don't you worry now. Jesse'll get your wife back for you." Then she looked down at the dogs. "Go with him, Finn."

The lab took off like he'd been shot out of a cannon. I followed after him, as Rusty explained to his wife that Jesse needed his help.

"A boat captain?" I asked Rusty, as we hurried across the lawn after the man and his dog.

"Jesse's kind of a private guy," Rusty explained. "We served in the Marines together—Force Recon—and he retired as a sniper instructor. After the Corps, he lived alone up on that island of his for many years. Like a hermit, trying to hide from some inner demon. Then he met a woman, Alexis Dubois, and he started to escape those demons. He went to a dark place when Alex was murdered on the night they got married. What he does now gives him purpose again. Well, that and Savannah and their kids."

I stopped Rusty and turned to face him. "What exactly does he *do*? It's obvious he's not just a charter captain and everyone inside seemed to know and accept that."

"What's Jesse do?" Rusty asked. "He fixes things. And right now, he's fixin' to put you and your missus back together. You been Graceless long enough, son."

When we caught up with Jesse, he was stepping down into an offshore fishing boat, with the name *Gaspar's*

Revenge on the stern. It was tied to a barge at the head of a long canal lined with boats, the engines rumbling with a low, throaty growl.

"Is this the boat you're using to get to your fast boat?" I asked, stepping down into the cockpit.

Jimmy came out of the boat's interior and looked up as Jesse climbed the ladder to the flybridge. "Everything's secure down here, man."

"Cast off," Jesse ordered.

Rusty and Jimmy untied the lines, as I just stood there. The big lab stood on his hind legs, paws on the gunwale, and barked twice at the two men.

"We're going as fast as we can, Finn," Rusty growled back.

"What can I do?" I called up to Jesse.

"Come on up," he replied. "For now, your phone is the only way we have to follow them."

Jesse sat down at the helm and switched on the chart plotter and radar. "Sit here in the second seat for now," he said.

Having just met the man and knowing next to nothing about him, it was plain to see that he was used to giving orders and having those orders obeyed. So, I did what I was told.

I took my phone out and looked at the tracker. There were two more pings, both in a line going from Key West up the outside of the Keys, toward Miami. The most recent one was a good fifteen miles up the Keys.

They were trying harder to access Grace's files.

Jimmy and Rusty jumped aboard as Jesse put the left controller into reverse and the boat slowly moved its bow away from the barge.

He looked at the tracker on my phone. "Good, they're still heading north. Any idea where they're going?"

"None," I replied. "But the most recent ping was just off Long Key a few minutes ago. They'll be near my house before long."

His phone rang, as he slowly navigated out of the little marina and into a channel cut through the shallows. He answered it, and listened for a moment, as Jimmy and Rusty joined us on the bridge. The two men sat on a bench seat on the left side of the boat, waiting.

"Head this way, and when you get close, turn around and stay ahead of them," Jesse said to whoever he was talking to on the phone. "You can always double back if they stop. But even with those Sevens on your Proline, you won't be able to catch the Tirranna. Neither will I if he makes a run."

He ended the call and pushed the throttles forward a little. I could see on the combination chart plotter that the water in the channel was only eight feet deep. I didn't know how much his boat's draft was, but I knew what would happen if he went to full throttle too soon. The back of the boat would sink as the bow came up, and maybe hit the bottom with one of the props. He'd have to wait for deeper water.

His phone rang again, but instead of answering it, he tapped the *Settings* icon and paired the phone with Bluetooth. The old-timey ringtone emanated from speakers mounted in the overhead console.

Jesse tapped the screen again and said, "What's *Ambrosia's* status Jack?"

"Just splashed her this morning," the man he called Jack replied, his voice smooth and articulate. "Matt and Heitor ran all the diagnostics and took her offshore just before sunset. *Ambrosia* is thirty miles off Miami right now, running up the turbines."

"Are you comfortable letting him make a night interception?" Jesse asked.

"To finally nail Franks and Hyde, yes."

"Todd Franks?" I asked, a bit bewildered.

It seemed like ages ago when I'd called CyberWard and talked to Grace's boss, but it'd only been a few days. I'd promised to keep him up to date on anything I learned.

"We're leaving Marathon now, Jack," Jesse said, glancing over at me. "Hyde's got a head start, they're off Long Key in a pair of go-fast boats. Top speed of sixty-two knots. They're running slower than that, out past the reef. Still, at the speed they're going, he'll have to stop for gas soon, if he doesn't reach his destination, and there aren't many places that have 91-octane."

"I already ordered Matt to move to intercept," Jack said. I assumed he was the employer Jesse had mentioned, Jack Armstrong. "*Ambrosia* will be off Key Largo in less than an hour and Chyrel's moving the satellite. She'll have eyes in fifteen minutes."

A satellite?

I looked over at the man beside me again. Jesse McDermitt was definitely not an ordinary fishing boat captain.

"We're on the way," he said, advancing the throttles as we got to deeper water. "Gotta go." He ended the call and pushed the throttles way forward.

The engines roared and G-forces pushed me back into my seat like some invisible hand against my chest. The boat accelerated like a sportscar, as Jesse made a wide turn around an island with dozens of townhomes and condos. I looked at the chart plotter. We were going forty knots—over forty-five miles per hour—curving around Key Colony Beach.

"Why are you doing this?" I yelled over the noise. "I mean, I understand what you said earlier about your wife being killed, but you don't know me from Adam."

"I know Reilly," Jesse shouted back. "I know he's careful and probably had you checked out nine ways to Sunday."

I shook my head in disbelief. "AJ and Reg on Grand Cayman, Boone and Emily on Cozumel, Buck and Ray in Key West, and now you guys. I don't get it. For all any of you know, I might be a drug smuggler chasing someone who stole my stash."

"Did you say Boone and Emily?" Jesse asked, glancing over at me with a grin. "A tiny English spitfire with a thing for green, and her boyfriend, a tall, wiry guy?"

"You know them?" I asked in surprise.

"Met them once," he replied, smiling broadly, and shaking his head. "Down near Saba, in the Lesser Antilles. They'd just blown up a narco-sub."

"Nah, can't be the same ones. These two are—"

"Divemasters?" Jesse finished. Coming out of the turn, but still inside the reef, Jesse reached for the throttles. "Hang on!"

I thought we were already going full speed when he pushed the twin throttles all the way forward. A high-pitched scream came from behind us and I was again pushed back in my seat.

Jesse waved to get Jimmy's attention, then pointed to his ear and held up four fingers. I knew basic hand signals for diving, but had no idea what he was communicating,

Jimmy rose and went down the ladder. When I looked at

the digital SOG indicator, our speed over ground was wavering at nearly fifty-five knots—over sixty miles per hour!

When he returned, Jimmy handed a little box to each of us. Jesse opened his, took a small device out, and showed it to me. He pushed and held a button on the side until a small red dot flashed twice. Then he put the device in his ear, looping a spring around the outside of his ear.

I did the same and when I stuck the thing in my ear, Jesse's voice came through it clearly with no background noise.

"Comm check."

"Loud and clear," Rusty responded.

Jimmy nodded. "Me, too, man."

Jesse looked at me and I said, "You're not really just a boat captain, are you?"

"Keep your eyes forward," he said by way of reply. "At this speed, the *Revenge* isn't all that maneuverable."

I looked straight ahead, suddenly fearful for anything in our path. "And this isn't just a fishing boat, either."

"*Gaspar's Revenge* is a tournament fisher," Jimmy said, sitting sideways on the bench, eyes forward. "We just took part in the Stock Island marlin tourney a few weeks back. Didn't win anything, but dude, it was a blast."

"Being the first one out to the fishing grounds don't always mean ya get the prize money," Rusty said.

"I didn't know sport fishers were this fast," I said.

"They're not," Jesse replied. "At least not most. The *Revenge* has a pair of Rolls Royce V-10s that we supercharged."

"Jesse are you on here?" a woman's voice with a decidedly Southern accent came over the ear bud.

"Hey, Chyrel," Jesse said. "Got anything?"

"I have them on the satellite feed," she replied. "A silver looking boat with six engines and a smaller yellow one with four. They're twenty-one nautical miles ahead of you. I've tagged them with IR and I'm sending their location to your chart plotter now."

I looked down at the plotter and a red dot appeared with a number beside it that bounced between 39.9 and 40.2. The dot was farther from the island chain than we were, probably outside the barrier reef.

"Got it," Jesse said. "They're running slow. Either to conserve fuel or because of the chop on the outside."

"At your closing speed," the woman said, "you'll intercept in a little over an hour. *Ambrosia's* underway and should be off North Key Largo before that. You should catch the targets off Tavernier."

"What's *Ambrosia*?" I asked, amazed at the technology these people had at their disposal.

Jesse glanced over and grinned. "If I told you, you wouldn't believe me. So, you'll just have to wait and see."

"Boat ahead," Rusty said, looking through a pair of binoculars. "Two miles, heading toward the reef."

"Got it," Jesse acknowledged, adjusting the wheel ever so slightly.

A deep baritone voice came over the little radio thing in my ear. "Bourke here. Tony's with me, and we're running south to intercept."

"Why's he running outside the reef?" yet another voice asked, this one decidedly African-American. "He could go a little faster on the inside and use the same amount of fuel."

"The ignorance of the average criminal has to be figured

in," Jesse said. "They probably don't know the waters as well."

"Speaking of which," Rusty said, as the boat he'd pointed out flashed past on the right. "Conrad Reef's just ahead."

Jesse made another slight course correction. I assumed the guy with the booming voice was the man Jesse had talked to on the phone. These people were putting things together so fast, and from so many places, that I in no way believed they were only regular citizens. Some sort of waterborne militia group? Whoever they were, they had very deep pockets.

I glanced over at Rusty and Jimmy. The bar owner was about Jesse's age, with a good bit of gray in his reddish beard. His head was shaved and he was a few pounds overweight. Though short in stature, the extra weight didn't seem to slow him any, but he didn't strike me as the law enforcement type.

Jimmy was thin and average height, with long hair and a sparse goatee on his chin. He looked about my age and my first thought was that he was a surfer. But there are few surfers in the Keys. There were just never any waves. He also didn't appear to be a cop.

Jesse, on the other hand, looked like a recruiting poster for the FBI or CIA. Having worked for DHS and the Marines before that, it was no wonder. His bearing and presence were a force to be reckoned with.

Jack Armstrong seemed to know all about, and had a great deal of interest in, Todd Franks and Stanley Hyde.

"I know this might sound like a really dumb question," I began. "But what can you tell me about my wife?"

Jesse glanced over and for a moment, nobody on the

communication device said anything. Finally, I heard the smooth voice of Jack Armstrong in my ear.

"Mr. Fitzgerald, that's probably something you need to talk to your wife about. I know you may be having all kinds of mixed feelings about what she does and how she's involved, but I *can* tell you this much—she's one of the good guys."

He knew a lot more about Grace than I did, that was obvious. We'd been together for twenty-three years. I knew everything about her that made her happy. I knew she liked honey in her morning coffee. I knew her favorite meal was fish tacos. I knew the spot on her neck that never failed to raise goosebumps all down her right arm. But this man, Jack Armstrong, knew more about what she did when she wasn't at home with me.

We all stared out at the calm water ahead. A powerful spotlight on the roof made an oval on the water a half mile in front of us and a half moon was slightly behind us, providing enough light to see the water quite well.

Jesse had to adjust course a couple more times, as his boat sped after the two go-fast boats, which I now realized was a bit of a misnomer. The boat with six engines, which Jesse had identified as a Cigarette Tirranna, had a top speed only five knots faster than we were currently going.

"Radar contact," the man named Bourke said. "We're stopping off Lower Matecumbe Key. If they decide to haul ass, we can't catch them."

"Bleddy good that we're almost on top o' the emmets, yeah?" a man's voice with a British accent said.

Jesse looked over at me and grinned. "Where are you, Matt?"

"Five miles off North Key Largo, Cap'n. Your orders?"

"Andrew and Tony will be in front of them and we'll be behind. The two boats are running outside the reef and we're inside. I want *Ambrosia* to circle around and come up on their starboard side, fully lit up, and force them toward the reef on my order."

"What do you want us to do?" Rusty asked.

Jesse looked over at his friend. "I want you and Jimmy to break out the mini-gun and take out their engines."

15

"I have facial recognition," Chyrel said, as Rusty and Jimmy disappeared down the ladder. "Both Todd Franks and Stanley Hyde are on the Cigarette. Still working on the two men in front, as well as the two on the other boat. I'll patch the satellite feed to your overhead monitor."

Jesse reached up and opened a door in the console above our heads, then he switched on what looked like a closed-circuit TV monitor. A boat appeared, barely lit by the moonlight, as it bounced over the waves.

"Hang on," Chyrel said. "Lemme zoom in and establish image stabilization…there, that oughta do it."

The bouncing of the boat stopped and the camera angle was like I was looking down on the boat's cockpit from an angle with the boat sitting still on a trailer and water splashing all around it. The people in the boat seemed to all be listening to the same music, their heads and arms were bouncing in synchronicity.

My eyes fell on Grace, sitting in back between two men.

Her hair streamed behind her and I could see what looked like blood on her shirt.

"That's Grace!" I yelled. "They hurt her."

My rage kicked in, adding more adrenaline to my already taxed system. Then I looked at the men on either side of her.

"That's him!" I said, pointing at the guy in the tropical shirt and slacks. He wasn't wearing the aviator shades, and his face was only slightly illuminated from the boat's interior lights, but I was sure of it. "The man in the back, wearing a tropical shirt. He's the guy who told me and Buck that he was an FBI agent named Foster. I don't know who any of the others are.

"The man in the fruit juicy shirt is Stanley Hyde," Chyrel said. "Formerly a special forces staff sergeant in the U.S. Army, now a known hitman. The other guy in the backseat is Todd Franks."

"But he's in California," I said. "And I saw Fost...er... Hyde get on the yellow boat."

"He must have switched boats," Jesse said.

"Todd Franks flew out of Palo Alto six days ago on his way to Haiti," Chyrel said. "And I just got a hit on the silver boat's driver. His name's Jason Newhall, a known associate of Hyde's. Last seen in the BVI where Hyde was reported entering a week ago, although nobody realized it for several days."

The voicemail from Grace's friend came screaming into my mind. Kim Robinson had said that the guy she'd recommended to help Grace bring the boat across, Brandon Wiles, had been found dead in his apartment in the British Virgin Islands.

"Hyde or that Newhall guy killed a man named

Brandon Wiles a week ago in the BVI," I blurted out. "Brandon was recommended by a friend of Grace's to crew the boat."

"I'd bet Newhall took the crewman's place to get aboard your boat," Jesse surmised. "When did Franks leave Haiti, Chyrel?"

"He cleared out from Port-au-Prince the next day," she replied.

"That was the last contact I had with Grace," I said. "They stopped for fuel at a marina there."

"That's likely where they made their move against her," Chyrel said. "And they got a computer person on board to try to access her files."

"Makin' our turn, Cap'n," the Englishman said over the little earbud. "We'll be abreast of you shortly, yeah?"

"Roger that," Jesse replied, leaning toward the chart plotter. "Got them on radar now. Three nautical miles ahead. We'll intercept in three minutes. I want you to turn on all your lights as you pass us. That should provide enough of a distraction that they might not notice us."

Ahead and to the right, way in the distance, I could just make out something moving on the water. I couldn't quite see what it was, but the whitewater it generated was huge. Then I saw navigation lights, red on the right and green on the left. It was a boat turning toward us and it was big.

"That's *Ambrosia*," Jesse said, seeing it, too.

The boat drew closer and closer, as the green light disappeared from view. I suddenly realized just how big it was, as it slowly fell past us, still turning—*Ambrosia* was a megayacht.

Coming out of a wide turn, about a mile away, I could

see the full length of it in the moonlight. Then all the lights came on.

Ambrosia was running parallel to us and though I couldn't believe it, was accelerating and passing us!

I noticed movement on Jesse's boat's long foredeck. Jimmy and Rusty had climbed out of a deck hatch and were doing something up near the pulpit.

These guys were certifiable. At sixty miles per hour, who the hell goes out on an open deck with no life vests or jack lines.

The massive yacht passed us, going at least ten knots faster than we were. That's when I heard the high-pitched whine from far across the water. The shriek was like a jet airplane with the afterburners lit.

"Tavernier Key ahead and just off to the left," Rusty said, as he sat on the bow looking through the binoculars.

Jesse looked to the right at the massive yacht missile. "Matt, do you see the Y marker light on your chart, just past Conch Reef? There's a really long break in the reef right after that. Force them through."

"Aye, Cap'n," he replied. "Too shallow for *Ambrosia*, innit?"

"Yeah, but they'll see the marker and maybe they won't know that."

We were almost abreast of the two go-fast boats and *Ambrosia* was slowing and turning in to cut them off.

"Andrew!" Jesse shouted needlessly. "Once they come inside the reef do something to distract their attention."

I could see the two boats clearly in the moonlight. First one, then the other, turned sharply to the left to avoid the big yacht bearing down on them.

"We're ready!" Jimmy yelled.

In the distance, I could see another boat going in the same direction as the targets. As the two boats crossed into the shallower, calmer water, the other boat was just a few hundred yards in front of them.

Suddenly a giant rooster tail shot up from the lead boat, the water arcing far behind it, even raining down on the two go-fast boats.

Andrew's distraction.

The two boats slowed and we were nearly on top of them, when Jesse shouted, "Light 'em up!"

Suddenly, a ripping sound split the air, as a narrow stream of what looked like flame came from the bow. Shell casings began to litter the deck and fly overboard by the hundreds as the gatling gun spat fire and bullets. The stream moved across the water like a serpent, sending geysers in the air with thousands of impacts.

The whip of fire found the back of the yellow boat and it immediately veered to the right and slowed to a dead stop.

Jesse pulled back gently on the throttles as we shot past the yellow boat.

The ripping sound came again and the fiery snake danced across the water as it sought out the boat Grace was on. Just as the whip found the back of the Tirranna, it raked across the stern, sending sparks and flames up in the air. Then it disappeared and the gun fell silent, as the Cigarette also came to a sudden stop, one of the engines on fire.

Jesse quickly pulled back on the throttles and turned toward the disabled boat, the bright spotlight zeroing in on it. Another light from *Ambrosia* fell on the Cigarette and a loud voice from a speaker could be heard across the water.

"This is Travis Stockwell with Homeland Security. Stand

and put your hands behind your head and prepare to be boarded!"

Jesse moved his boat closer, as the smaller boat that shot the rooster tail turned and came back toward us, adding a third powerful spotlight on the Cigarette.

Hyde held Grace with an arm locked around her neck and a gun at her head.

"Don't come any closer, or the woman dies!"

Jesse reached up and toggled a switch on the radio, then he held the mic to his mouth. "Go ahead. We know she's in on the leaked information. You have no way out of this, Hyde!"

Leaked information?

"What are you doing?" I said. "Grace isn't a part of any of this. If she was, she could open the information on her computer and they're still trying."

"They don't know that we know that," Jesse said quietly. Then he looked down at the foredeck. "Give them a warning splash, Jimmy."

Once more, the ripping fire spit out from the bow, sending a line of geysers along the side of the boat.

Thirty yards ahead, everyone in the Cigarette dropped below the gunwale. When the gun stopped, they slowly stood up, putting their hands behind their heads.

"Throw your guns in the water!" Jesse commanded over the PA speaker.

One by one, the men on the boat did as they were told.

"Good choice," Jesse said. "Now all five of you move up to the bow. Get on your knees, with your ankles crossed and face the big boat out past the reef."

One by one, even Grace, they went forward and knelt on the deck.

"Tie off and board the boat, Andrew," Jesse said, then he turned to me. "It's almost over, Nathan. Why don't you go down to the swim platform and collect your wife? Andrew and Tony will bring her over in just a minute before they take the bad guys out to *Ambrosia*."

EPILOGUE

It'd been two days since Grace and I got back home. Jesse's friends brought her to his boat, with Hyde, Franks, and the other men, bound and lying on the deck. Then it had sped off toward the yellow boat to pick up the last two men and take them all out to the mega-yacht *Ambrosia*, sitting out beyond the reef.

He never told me what would happen to them and I never asked.

Jesse had then taken us to Tavernier Creek Marina, where another person on his team, a guy named Paul, drove us the few blocks to Mariner's Hospital. He'd even waited and taken us home after Grace had been checked out.

The doctor didn't find anything physically wrong with her, so I asked her about the blood on her shirt.

"It's not mine," Grace said, as we got into Paul's car. "One of those hired thugs got a little too close and I punched him. His nose sprayed blood like a fountain."

We'd slept past noon the next day, with the drapes

closed tightly against the bright sunlight. I'd told Grace a little about what had happened but went into more detail over a late lunch at The Hideout on Largo Sound.

It was then that I'd remembered I'd promised to call AJ on Grand Cayman and Boone and Emily on Cozumel. When I'd called AJ first, she was very happy to hear the news and had told me that Boone and Emily were actually with her. She'd put her phone on speaker and we talked to the three of them for a few minutes. It seemed that the Cozumel couple were looking into shifting their dive op to the Cayman Islands.

After that, I'd called Buck Reilly in Key West. I'd felt bad about what happened to his plane, but he'd said he'd been planning to do a complete rebuild for a long time and was already taking steps to have a guy in Marathon bring it back by barge for Ray to get started on it.

When we'd called Jesse after that, we found out who the friend was. The big barge his boat had been tied to was owned by his friend Rusty and it was being prepped to move Buck's plane. Before we ended the call, Jesse invited us down to Marathon to celebrate. When I asked what, he'd said that he'd learned that Grace was being promoted to fill a recent management vacancy.

Grace hadn't heard anything about it, but Jesse assured us it was a done deal. So, we'd agreed to drive down the following day.

Grace's phone rang the following morning, as we sat on the porch watching the sun come up, before driving down to Marathon.

She looked at the screen and said, "It's CyberWard."

"Put it on speaker," I told her.

She did and then said hello.

"Good morning, Ms. Fitzgerald," a woman said. "This is Janet Acrivos, personal assistant to the president of CyberWard. I hope I didn't wake you. How are you feeling today?"

"You didn't," Grace said, leaning over the phone. "And I'm fine, thank you."

"Would you mind holding just a moment for Mr. Sutton."

"Sure," Grace said.

There was a click and she looked up at me. "Frank Sutton founded CyberWard."

Over the last couple of days, Grace had told me more about her work and how she'd suspected Todd Franks of leaking secret files to foreign governments. Files that had to do with cyber security. Although he'd had access to the files, the key to opening them was on her laptop.

"Grace," a man's voice came over the phone. "Frank Sutton here. I do hope you weren't hurt too badly. I feel terrible about what happened."

"I was just smacked around a little," she said. "They knew they couldn't hurt me badly."

"At any rate, I'm sorry it happened and doubly so since you'd been the one to actually predict it. To that end, I've decided how to repay you for your loyalty and hard work. Would you consider taking over Todd Franks's position? It really should be someone who can speak the language to the tech people anyway. We can't locate Franks anywhere."

"Senior Cyber Security Manager?" she asked, surprise written all over her face.

"It comes with a substantial raise in salary," he said. "You'll continue to work remotely, and to sweeten the pot, I've arranged the delivery of a three-year-old, barely used,

Bavaria C38. Say the word and I'll have the boat brought to whatever marina you choose."

While she talked, I pulled up the specs on the C38. It had three cabins and was one of the nominees for sailing yacht of the year by Sail Magazine in 2018. It was worth three or four times what we'd paid for *Anegada da Vida*.

Grace asked if she could call him back later, that we were just on our way out the door, and she wanted to discuss it with me before making a decision. He agreed and they ended the call.

"I'm going to take it," she said, as we walked out to the car. "What I want to know is how that guy in Marathon knew before Mr. Sutton even called me."

"Having seen what he was able to pull together in short order, I don't think there's much of anything he can't find out."

We drove south on Overseas Highway, while listening to the radio. Neither of us said much.

"One thing still confuses me," I said, glancing over at Grace.

"What's that?"

"When I was in the plane with Buck and we flew over you, I'm sure I saw a gun in your hand."

"Todd was paranoid," she said. "He gave me an unloaded gun and forced me to point it at the airplane. I guess he wanted it to look like I was in on the security theft."

"I knew it had to be something like that," I said. There was no way I was ever going to tell her that I'd doubted her.

We drove on in awkward silence for a while.

"I'm sorry I didn't tell you more about what I do," Grace finally said.

"And I'm sorry I didn't ask. It's just that all that techno-talk is foreign to me. I'm just a washed-up ball player trying to keep a few high school kids on the straight and narrow."

"You're a lot more than that, Nathan, and you know it. If it hadn't been for you, they would have eventually gotten my files open and then I'd have been useless to them."

"Take the job, Grace," I said. "You're good at what you do. He wouldn't make the offer if you weren't."

She called Sutton back and accepted the offer, as I drove through the town of Layton on Long Key. They talked for a few minutes and agreed on a conference video call in two days, between the two of them and the team of specialists who'd be working under her.

When we passed the Marathon airport, I pointed out the Grumman Jesse owned and was surprised to see both of Buck's airplanes parked right beside it. I was also surprised to see the propellers spinning on Jesse's plane and people getting out of it. I made a U-turn then pulled into the long driveway by the leaning mailbox.

"This is pretty," Grace said, as the dense foliage swallowed the car.

"Yeah, it's like a little jungle."

Looking around, I didn't see Jesse's old truck. Parking close to the building, we got out, and went to the front door.

I glanced at my watch. "We're a little early," I said, pulling the door open.

"Well, ain't you a sight for sore eyes," Rusty said, coming out from behind the bar. He gave me and Grace both a hug, then looked closely at her. "You prolly don't remember me. I'm Rusty Thurman, owner of the Rusty Anchor."

"It's good to see you again," Grace said.

"Where's Jesse and Jimmy?" I asked.

"Jesse's out back. He and Savannah are talking to my cook, Rufus," he replied, leading us to the bar. "And Jimmy took his truck to run to the airport real quick. What can I get you to drink? On the house."

Just then, Jesse came in through the back door. He saw us and smiled. "I wasn't expecting you for another hour."

"How did you know?" Grace said, as Jesse's wife Savannah came in with a little boy.

"Know what?"

"About my promotion," Grace said. My boss only called me this morning.

"I told him," a woman sitting at the bar said. "Good to finally meet y'all."

She was smallish, with short, wavy, blond hair. And her accent was pure Alabama.

"Chyrel?" I asked.

Grace turned suddenly to face her. "Ms. Koshinski?"

She smiled, stepped down from her stool, then hugged Grace tightly. "I'm so glad you're okay."

"But how?" Grace stammered.

I was completely confused.

"It was me who recommended you," Chyrel said.

"Grace," Jesse said, "I'd like you to meet my wife, Savannah, and our son, Alberto."

They shook hands and we all sat down at a big table. Chyrel and Grace went on to explain how Chyrel had done a lot of consulting work for CyberWard and how Armstrong Research relied on them for cyber security.

The front door opened and Jesse looked up with a grin. "Looks like the rest of the guests are here."

I looked over and saw Buck Reilly coming through the door with Ray Floyd. Then Jimmy opened the door and held it while several others came in, the first being Emily Durand and her boyfriend, Boone Fischer. Right behind them were AJ Bailey and the Caymanian constable, Nora Sommer, who was even smiling. AJ's friend, Reg Moore, brought up the rear.

Emily scurried across the room, as Jesse stood up. "Stretch Buchannan, blimey it's good to see you again," she said, as he bent over to accept a hug.

"Miss Durand," Jesse said, then nodded at her boyfriend, extending a hand. "Boone, how've you been?"

"Stretch Buchannan?" I asked, as the two men shook.

The confusion must have been apparent on my face.

"Sorry," Jesse said, then turned to Boone and Emily. "Stretch isn't my real name. It's Jesse McDermitt."

Emily shoved Boone. "Exactly what I told you, yeah?"

More introductions were made and more people arrived. The barrel-chested Andrew and his friend Tony, as well as the Englishman Matt Brand, who'd commanded *Ambrosia*.

AJ and Emily looked at one another, grinning, when he spoke and AJ said, "Looks like another English invasion."

"Oye, I'm not English, mate," Matt said, with a grin. "Once you cross the River Tamar, you're no longer in England."

I looked around the table at everyone, as the banter flew back and forth. They were people from all over and from different walks of life. Yet, they'd all helped me to get my wife back.

Rusty was staring at me curiously, so I leaned over the table toward him. "I still don't get it. Grace and I are just regular people, nobodies really. Why would you and all these others risk your lives to help us?"

"One human family, man," Jimmy said, sitting next to him.

"He's sorta right," Rusty said. "I live on this island and my family's been here for over a hundred years." The talk around the table faded, as he went on. "People have always been drawn to these 'islands in the stream' and some put down roots."

He looked over at Jesse and continued. "Jesse and Savannah live on a different island." He grinned at him. "We met on an island—Parris Island." His gaze turned from one person to another. "Buck and Ray, they live on a different island, these young folks from still other islands, and you and your wife on yet one more."

"I'm tellin' ya, dude," Jimmy insisted. "One. Human. Family."

"We're all islanders," Rusty summarized. "You, too. Whether here, or Cayo Hueso, or Coz, or Grand, or Largo, we all stick together. It's the island way. You step on one of our toes, and a whole bunch of islanders from all over will rise up and say *ouch*."

The End

If you enjoyed *Graceless*, you'll love *Timeless*,
a full-length novel by the same four authors.
Discover more books in the genre, and sign up for the
newsletter with new releases and great deals at
www.TropicalAuthors.com

AFTERWORD PART I
BY NICHOLAS HARVEY

Author of the AJ Bailey Adventure Series and
the Nora Sommer Caribbean Suspense Series

Nicholas wrote the opening chapters set in Key Largo and Grand Cayman.

From the very beginning *Graceless* created its own momentum.

Spawned from a Zoom call Wayne Stinnett put together, discussing ways to grow the Tropical Authors group, the idea of a collaborative novella was raised—a story that travelled through the realms of our protagonists.

I was in the middle of writing book 10 in my AJ Bailey series, starting a prequel novella for my Nora Sommer series, and plotting Nora's first novel. But I stopped everything. I couldn't sleep. I was obsessed with this story as it slowly fell into my mind. I imagined a logical path around the Caribbean, hitting the wonderful locations we all write about. That created an obvious order for the authors; The Cayman Islands, Cozumel, Key West, and Marathon.

The first problem was how to visit all these locations and introduce our characters. Nathan was conceived, and he would travel around the Caribbean in search of his missing wife. I'd never written in first person before, but it was the obvious way to observe all our characters and locations, using one man's perspective. I'd also never written in US English, as I'm from the UK. I wrote my part in two days and sent it to Nick Sullivan.

Nick is always busy. He's either narrating, writing, acting or walking his dog, Momo. He said he'd take a look on a trip to see his family in a week or so, and maybe tackle his writing part in a month. He called me the very next day, full of ideas to start his section. Momentum.

We devised a system. The previous author(s) and the next author up had a Zoom meeting. We talked about the storyline and how we each envisioned it progressing. We left breadcrumbs for the next writer to pick up and run with. There were only three rules for me, Nick, and John; don't kill Nathan (as he provides the narrative), Grace (as there'd be no one to look for), or the dog—because you never, ever kill the dog. When the story reached Wayne, he only had rule three, everyone else was fair game!

A project that began as a long-term plan—whenever we could squeeze it in—took four authors just six weeks to complete the first draft. Momentum. *Graceless* took on a life of its own. A logical geographic path naturally fed the escalating storyline with each new author. Everyone contributed their own style, yet the story read as though one author penned every word.

What a pleasure it has been working with three great writers I respect and admire. I felt like an apprentice studying at the feet of the masters.

ABOUT THE AUTHOR

Nicholas Harvey's life has been anything but ordinary. Race car driver, mountaineer, divemaster, and since 2019 a full-time novelist. Raised in England, Nick now lives next to the ocean in Key Largo with his amazing wife, Cheryl.

Motorsports may have taken him all over the world, both behind the wheel and later as a Race Engineer and Team Manager, but diving inspires his destinations these days – and there's no better diving than in Grand Cayman where Nick's AJ Bailey Adventure and Nora Sommer Caribbean Suspense series are based.

Drawing from his own thirst for adventure, experience

underwater, and a lifetime of storytelling, Nick's novels put you right in the middle of the action. Feel the ocean breeze brushing your face, the warm water washing over your feet, and the villains chasing you across the tropical island!

Find out more info and join his newsletter at
www.HarveyBooks.com

AFTERWORD PART II
BY NICK SULLIVAN

Author of The Deep Series

Nick wrote the chapters set in Cozumel.

Several years ago, I began a multi-author project with a group of fellow authors and narrators, and we created several fascinating pieces. The intention was to record them as an episodic audio experience, but life got in the way, and the Round Robin project went fallow. Then, earlier this year, a random suggestion during a business meeting brought another opportunity! Back in 2019 I created Tropical Authors, a site for authors who set their books on the water, near the water, under the water, along the coast, or on tropical islands. True "beach reads." As I write this, we have thirty-nine writers!

Several of our members have been part of TA from early on, and four of us decided to have a Zoom Meeting to brainstorm on where we wanted the group to go. Nicholas Harvey, Wayne Stinnett, John H. Cunningham, and I had a conversation about the frequency of the Tropical Authors newsletters, briefly discussed selling "swag" on the website, and were moving on to other topics when Nicholas Harvey suggested "Why don't we… write something… together." Boom. Everyone pounced with ideas and suggestions, and within minutes the meeting became about this new venture. Everyone was "all in." Heck, before we were done, we were already fantasizing about the other authors in the group doing their own Tropical Authors Novellas. We talked about when we might be able to come up with a first draft for this four-part novella, and I remember hearing "Maybe Labor Day?" Heh. It happened a lot faster than that.

Mere days after the meeting, Nicholas Harvey sent me the opening to the book. A quick aside here… having a pair of "Nicks" can get confusing. Since Harvey's from the UK and I'm from Tennessee, we sometimes sign our emails "Brit Nick" and "Hick Nick." What Brit Nick handed over was a wonderfully sculpted opening act. I should point out that the hardest part of writing is the beginning… and in this case, Nicholas had to create a brand new "everyman" character who could travel through our respective worlds, and then plop him down into a situation that left numerous pathways for the three of us to exploit. I must say, it was a masterful set-up. As I read it, ideas popped into my mind with every passing page.

My next Deep Series book is set in the Cayman Islands, but fortunately (in my fictional timeline) Boone and Emily were still in Book Four's location of Cozumel. After Brit Nick sent the sailboat my way, I was eager to jump in; I ended up writing my entire section in about a week while visiting family. One aspect of this exercise was truly enjoyable: writing in first person. I've only done it once, in that Round Robin project I mentioned, and that was years ago. Since The Deep Series follows both Boone Fischer and Emily Durand, my books contain frequent point-of-view shifts between them, and third person worked best. Having the opportunity to follow Nathan—an outside observer—as he interacted with Boone and Em, allowed me to describe their appearance and personalities in ways I'd never been able to do!

There were several plot points that Nicholas set up that offered multiple possibilities: Agent Foster... he *could* be an FBI agent... but maybe not. Grace... what was she *really* doing for a living? And who exactly had taken the sailboat? I decided, with two authors to go—and both of them being top-notch action-adventure, thriller writers—that I should leave many of these plot points open-ended and toss it their way, figuring they would run with it. Oh boy, did they.

As my section came to a close, I came up with a way for Nathan to track Grace... and the ball was tossed to John H. Cunningham and his treasure-hunting adventurer, Buck Reilly!

ABOUT THE AUTHOR

Born in East Tennessee, Nick Sullivan has spent most of his adult life as an actor in New York City, working in theater, television, film, and audiobooks. After recording hundreds of books over the last twenty years he decided to write some of his own. An avid scuba diver for many years, his travels to numerous Caribbean islands have inspired The Deep Series (formerly Caribbean Dive Adventures). *Deep Shadow* is set on the Dutch island of Bonaire and its sequel, *Deep Cut*, is set on the little island of Saba. Book Three, *Deep Roots*, takes place in Belize, Book Four, *Deep Devil*, takes Boone Fischer and Emily Durand up the coast to Cozumel, and Book Five, *Deep Focus*, is set in the Cayman Islands.

Visit www.nicksullivan.net or www.deepnovels.com for social media links, and to sign up for the author's mailing list.

AFTERWORD PART III
BY JOHN H CUNNINGHAM

Author of the Buck Reilly Adventure Series

John wrote the chapters set in Key West.

When the day came for our Zoom call to brainstorm how to grow Tropical Authors, I was running late, sitting with artist David Wegman at his home in Key West discussing the short film I had written that he was starring in, called *Flight to Life*. When I realized what time it was, I dialed up Zoom from my phone and joined Wayne Stinnett, Nick Sullivan (Hick Nick) and Nicholas Harvey (Brit Nick) mid-discussion. Wayne had suggested the call, and when Wayne has an idea, it's always interesting.

We caught up, and the brainstorming began, which led to Brit Nick ultimately posing the idea that we collaborate on a novella. Aside from the film, I was wrapping up book #9 in the Buck Reilly series, *Indigo Abyss*, plus working my day job as Regional Director of New York City for a major real estate investment trust, so I hesitated, mentally, for a second, but was then totally pulled in by the opportunity to collaborate with three of my favorite authors and people I both like and admire. Plus, it would happen somewhere in the distant future, "when we all had time to work on it..."

The future often comes at you faster than you expect, as it was only a couple weeks later that I got a note from Nick Harvey saying that he'd finished the opening section of what he'd suggested we call *Graceless*, and was now handing it off to Nick Sullivan. Then, within maybe a week, Nick Sullivan was done, and they wanted to schedule a call with me to discuss the basics of the story, which aside from me not killing Nathan, Grace or the dog, it was totally up to me what happened next. Sounds easy, right? Not. Many writers are what they refer to as "pantsers" because they write by the seat of their pants—including a couple of my collaborators on *Graceless*. However, I am a painstaking outliner who likes to think through many details before even starting a story, but here it was, already half done and I was seeing it for the first time.

When I read the first two sections, I was totally sucked in and dropped everything to start my part. I'd taken notes of all the details, characters, places and story arc, then jotted down a few notes for where I wanted it to go next, and dove in. Nathan had already been through hell searching for his missing wife Grace in Grand Cayman and Cozumel, but the trail had now led to Key West and Buck Reilly, who along with several characters from my series, jumped in, cautiously at first, but then rallied to help this virtual stranger find the truth, as painful as that might be. Turned out to be very painful for Buck, but where his opportunity to help crashed and burned, it was fortunately close to where Wayne Stinnett has set much of his series. Enter Jesse McDermitt and his crack team to bring *Graceless* home. What a fun ride it was to work with these authors and produce this breathless romp through the Caribbean!

ABOUT THE AUTHOR

John H. Cunningham is the author of the best-selling, Key West based, nine book, Buck Reilly Adventure Series. John has either lived in or visited the many locations that populate his novels, and he mixes fact with fiction and often includes real people in the cast of characters. Adhering to the old maxim, "write what you know," John's books have an authenticity and immediacy that have earned a loyal following and strong reviews. John writes stories that concern themselves with the same tensions and issues that affect all of our lives, and his choices for the places and plots that populate his stories include many settings that he loves, including Key West, Cuba, Jamaica, and multiple Caribbean locations. John is also an Executive Vice President, and Regional Director of New York City for a public Real Estate Investment Trust. He splits his time between New York, Virginia and Key West.

Visit www.jhcunningham.com to learn more, or to sign up for John's newsletter and social media links.

AFTERWORD PART IV
BY WAYNE STINNETT

Author of the
Jesse McDermitt Caribbean Adventure Series,
the Charity Styles Caribbean Thriller Series,
and the DJ Martin and Jerry Snyder Caribbean Mystery Series

Wayne wrote the chapters set in Marathon.

In the spring of 2021, Nick Sullivan and I were talking on the phone about marketing ideas for our Tropical Authors group. No, that wasn't the purpose of the call, it was just something that came up in passing. We decided on a "steering committee" for the group to discuss ideas. Besides the two of us, we included Nicholas Harvey, who was already helping Nick with the Tropical Authors newsletter, and John H. Cunningham, with his brilliant business mind.

Through email, the four of us chose a date and set up a Zoom Meeting to discuss marketing ideas. The four of us are boaters and scuba divers, and over the years, we've become good friends. There were a lot of great ideas tossed around, then Nick (island Nick, Nick of the South, Brit Nick… Nicholas Harvey) said something about writing a reader magnet novella.

I'd done one of these before with another group of authors. But not as a reader magnet, just as a way of bringing some cheer to a friend who was going through bad times. It was fun and rewarding. That one involved about a dozen authors and took half a year. So, I wasn't holding my breath that Brit Nick's idea would come to fruition any time soon.

Then it did.

In just a matter of a few weeks, *Graceless* was born. Brit Nick came up with a way we could each highlight our own characters in a different way. I write in first person point of view, so the only time I get to describe Jesse McDermitt is when he looks in the mirror and actually thinks about what he looks like. In 21 Jesse novels, that's only happened once. But he has crossed over into Charity's world a couple of times, so I was able to do it from her point of view and it was a lot of fun.

We had another Zoom Meeting, where we did a basic outline and set down a few rules, but by then, Brit Nick was almost finished with the opening quarter and ready to hand it off to Hick Nick. Yeah, we had to come up with childish *Nick*names (see what I did there?) for the two in the group with the same name, since Nicholas Harvey prefers to go by Nick and Nick Sullivan is a Tennessean. We tried just Hick and Brick, but that seemed a bit demeaning.

In that second Zoom Meeting, we first decided to have this new character, Nathan, move through our four worlds in a geographical way that made sense. He'd be a visitor and we'd each write separate parts, all in first person, so Nathan could reflect on the characters he meets and describe what he thinks about them. Geographically, our characters are flung across South Florida and the Caribbean. But Brit Nick devised the perfect plot vehicle to move Nathan through our worlds. He was looking for his wife, Grace—lost at sea—and the first clue pointed toward the Cayman Islands, where he found another clue that took him on to Cozumel, Mexico, then Key West, Florida, and finally, Marathon, Florida. As luck would have it, our characters in that same order had more and more confrontation with the bad guys and brought escalating abilities to handle them.

Being a mutual admiration group—all of us having read all of each other's works—we were able to lead each other into the next part of the story in a way that made it seem like one continuous story by a single author. It was a lot of fun working with these guys, whom I consider the cream of the crop of today's Tropical Authors. Wait, that's not quite true. There are a lot of other equally talented authors in our group of about forty, but instead of a novella, this would have become an epic tome of massive proportions.

But don't be surprised if another foursome in our motley crew doesn't pick up on this and start running with it. There may even be a sequel to *Graceless*.

ABOUT THE AUTHOR

Wayne Stinnett is an American author of more than twenty-five novels and one non-fiction book on writing. He's also a Veteran of the United States Marine Corps, as is his main character, Jesse McDermitt. Between those careers, Stinnett has worked as a deckhand, commercial fisherman, dive master, taxi driver, construction manager, and truck driver, among many other things. Currently, he's expanding his self-publishing company, Down Island Publishing, LLC, and is now publishing other authors' works, as well as continuing his own writing.

He lives with his wife and youngest daughter in the South Carolina Lowcountry. They also have three grown children, four grandchildren, a crazy Carolina dog, and a large cage full of parakeets. He grew up in Melbourne, Florida, and has also lived in the Florida Keys, the Bahamas, and Cozumel, Mexico, among other places.

Stinnett still gets down to Florida regularly, but more often than not, it's via his imagination and writing. All his books are set primarily in the Keys and around the Caribbean. His stories revolve around a retired Marine who is a charter boat captain living on an island in the Middle Keys, where he explores, dives, and fishes the back country of Florida Bay, the Gulf of Mexico, the Florida Straits, and all around the Caribbean Sea. That is until trouble comes looking for him.

Find out more info and join his newsletter at
www.waynestinnett.com.